"Explain,"
said the interrogation machine.
"Describe their culture."

"They have an important celebration," said E.T., "called Hollow Bean. Everyone carves faces in fruit squashes and dresses up in sheets."

"Who holds this celebration?"

"The children, who actually rule the Blue Planet of Earth. They are more intelligent than the older people and outrun them on bicycles."

The machine whirled around him again. "And what is the purpose of this celebration?"

"To collect the all-important food."

"Which is?"

"Candy."

E.T.

THE BOOK OF
THE GREEN
PLANET

a new novel by
WILLIAM KOTZWINKLE
based on a story by
STEVEN SPIELBERG

BERKLEY BOOKS, NEW YORK

E.T.
THE BOOK OF THE GREEN PLANET

A Berkley Book / published by arrangement with
MCA Publishing, a Division of MCA, Inc.

PRINTING HISTORY
Berkley edition / March 1985

ISBN: 0-425-07642-3

E.T.
THE BOOK OF
THE GREEN
PLANET

"Catch it! Maintain contact!"

Interceptor jets had scrambled and were laying plumes of exhaust on the horizon as they streaked upward.

The spaceship gained steadily, withdrawing itself with a calm dignity, its gleaming spherical form seeming to move with no effort through the heavens, while the jet planes strained at the edge of the atmosphere, shuddered, and turned their silver noses slowly over in defeat. The chase was abandoned, the ship beyond them now, rising still faster, a fading dot in the sky.

The Earth grew still smaller as E.T. gazed from his porthole, his heart heavy at the sight of its diminishing shape, which fell like a blue-white tear drop, lost in the void. His friends were there—Elliott and Michael, Mary and Gertie, and Harvey the dog, and he would never see them again. "Goodbye," he whispered in a hoarse croak, "goodbye."

The tear drop vanished, swallowed by space. He stared dully out of the porthole for a long time, his mind automatically arranging and filing all that he knew of Earth, principally its language, which he'd nearly mastered, thanks to Elliott. He had chug-a-lugged the words, and could tee off any number of them, like a real shot-hot.

But words, and the lyrics to a few rocks and rolling songs were all he had. And a geranium.

He turned toward it. It was small, almost insignificant in the vast, wild array of growing things that filled his section of the ship. He picked up the geranium and busied himself with it, making a place for it among the other plants of Earth that had been gathered; he made a tag for it, which, instead of saying *Geranium* said *Gertie*, a label that would cause some confusion in the Galactical Encyclopedia, but he didn't care. "B. good," he said, stroking the leaves, and continued on his rounds, among the other plants.

The Botanical Wing was the principal section of the ship, a huge dome hung with plants from every world, their foliage spilling down in lush profusion. The sloping walls were lined with tiers, on which more plants rested, bearing every possible kind of blossom, gaudy or discreet, delicate or ferociously armored—all of them feeding on nutrient tubes from below, or nutrient beakers slowly dripping from above. Soft lights, corresponding to suns of many hues, filtered by atmospheres as diverse as the planets themselves, played upon countless petals.

E.T. moved among them, through a collection he knew intimately, from the many worlds to which he'd traveled. The plants, exquisitely sensitive, knew him too, and perceived that a deep sadness had fallen on their beloved attendant, the celebrated Doctor of Botany.

Another such scholar of plant life entered the Botanical Wing, shuffling on webbed feet like E.T.'s. His head too was large and wrinkled, with soulfully searching eyes, and his body like E.T.'s was squat, with long arms that allowed his hands to touch the floor as he walked. And he saw that E.T. was sad and somber. He'd seen it before, when a planet of lovely vegetation like Earth's was left behind—some member of the staff would fall into melancholy. He shuffled over to E.T., and put his hand on E.T.'s shoulder. He spoke softly, in the language of their home planet, a soft, rasping sound. The syllables of his speech were infinitely subtle and refined, but roughly translated they meant, "Earth is not the only garden in the universe."

E.T. looked out of the porthole into empty space, and a name from the language of Earth broke from his wrinkled mouth. "Elliott!"

The other botanist looked around and scratched his head. No plant by that name had been brought on board. "What is the matter?" he asked E.T.

E.T. turned from the porthole and gazed at his colleague. A look of deep longing crossed his face, as his lips parted again. "Wiped . . . out."

Wiped out? The other old botanist ran the phrase through his memory bank of classic galaxy languages, but no connection was forthcoming, except for an image of someone drying the inside of a pot. Was his scientific brother sentimental over dishware?

"Stay here," he said, "with the Earth plants." He indicated the Earth section of the collection. "It will make you feel better."

E.T. remained as bidden, in the Earth section. He petted all the plants there, and crooned softly to them. He put his nose in their blossoms, to keep the memory of Earth alive, but it was just a memory and that is not quite the same thing at all.

* * *

The ship sped on, through Orion's belt, through the three star-pearls hanging there, hues now white, now yellow and purple. The ship altered its course, the plane changed and Orion's symmetry was lost. E.T. watched from his porthole, as Earth's solar system fell behind, the sun shifting to the red spectrum and becoming no more than a tiny glowing star. Now Elliott's world was irretrievable.

The other old botanist came up beside him again, his gaze following E.T.'s toward the vanishing solar system they'd visited. "But what did you do there that was so wonderful?"

"Ate candy."

E.T. rested his chin on the rim of the porthole and continued staring at the tiny sun, now but one of many suns in the Milky Way. The other old botanist shook his head and walked off.

E.T. turned back to the internal garden of the ship, to those flower beds at the center of the Wing, their circular pattern crowned by a bubbling fountain of nutrients. A Whistling Ertmog, from a planet in the Andromeda Galaxy, whistled at him. He stopped beside the little plant, whose whistling call was meant to attract the tiny birds who pollinated it. It warbled to him, singing its plaintive five-note tune.

Cheer up, its song seemed to say, and the other plants in the central beds joined in, their waves of concern flowing over him.

"I made a true friend on Earth," he told the plants. "He saved my neck." And he raised his neck to its full height, to show the plants just how much saving it had taken. "We went through all kinds of doodleysquat together."

It was important he practice Earth language in the proper fashion, so as to speak like a sophisticated and learned thingamajig.

The door to the Botanical Wing opened, and a Micro Tech entered, on his regular check of the Wing's mechanical functions. Like all Micro Techs, he was very small, about fifteen centimeters from head to toe. His body was nearly transparent, and his internal energy could be seen flowing and darting, highly charged. His hands were his most peculiar feature, for the fingers were as tiny and numerous as hairs, and each hair could do microscopically detailed work. He popped a panel in the wall of the chamber, and examined the intricate nest of electrical contacts, his fingers wriggling about and emitting tiny energic beeps. He closed the panel and moved to another one. His eyes were enormous, and his face like a marble, smooth and shiny. He looked at E.T.

"Well, you're in trouble. Plenty of it."

E.T. groaned. The Micro Tech sped up a ladder, to the center of the botanical dome, where he opened more panels, their interior lights winking on as he tested the solar-simulation circuitry for the hanging green world. He managed to look down at E.T. again.

"Tsk, tsk, tsk, certainly in trouble."

"Finish your business," scolded the other botanist, and then put his long arm around E.T.'s shoulder. "Pay no attention to him."

E.T. watered his geranium, and continued his lethargic rounds of the central beds. A long tongue emerged from a lush blossom and wrapped itself around his finger, as if he were the pollen-bearing insect desired by the plant. It was Lizard's Love from the jungles of planet Crees, and it had considerable affection for E.T., for he had been the one to bring it to the ship and care for it. Gently, he unwound its petal-tongue from his finger. "I'm in trouble," he said softly. And then, remembering a phrase that Mary used when things went wrong, he added, "I'm in the soup."

We don't care, said all the plants in unison. *You are the best.*

He opened their nutrient valve and shuffled back to his porthole.

"We are approaching the Dragon River of Stars," he said to the plants. "Within it is the Whirlpool of Time—first gate of dimension. The ship is already preparing for entry."

He watched as it began to enter the hole in space by which the universes were bridged. He felt the ship's entry, into the Whirlpool. In another moment they would leave this continuum for another, and he would have lost Elliott forever, which was worse than being in the soup.

*   *   *

They emerged like a genie from a bottle, their ship appearing from the void, into another universe.

"Through a series of such whirlpools, we shall eventually reach our home," said the other old botanist, E.T.'s only friend—for by this time, E.T. had discovered that he'd been screened off from the rest of the crew.

"Heart-lights are veiled," he said.

"Do not despair," said his friend.

But few words were exchanged outside of the Botanical Wing. E.T. wandered the ship, from quarter to quarter, looking for a game of checkers, which he'd learned on Earth, but no one would play.

In his loneliness, he finally carried his homemade checkerboard into the Micro Tech section—the power center of the ship. Here at the central reactor, the power was tempered by a company of the little beings, their millions of fingers everywhere.

He held up his checkerboard. The Micro Techs all stopped their work, and a hush descended in the power center. Then with one voice they all said, "Tsk, tsk, tsk," and went back to work.

* * *

"Napish Utim, the Veil of Stars."

The portholes of the ship flashed with rich pulsing colors from the whirling rainbow of brilliant gases. No member of the crew was indifferent to the sight, the portholes all filled, sighs of wonder echoing from them. E.T. shuffled slowly by, head down, carrying Gertie's geranium.

"Look!" cried a shipmate, as a newborn comet suddenly vaporized beside them, tail shooting forth in a glorious burst of light.

E.T. blinked. He saw, not the blazing ice and rock of the comet, but a boy's face, light-years away, trillions of miles behind him. "El-li-ott," he croaked.

From the innermost centers of his mind and soul, a wave of telepathic intensity was released, piercing the wall of the spaceship and the walls of time. It went down through Andromeda, between Aries and Pegasus, and into the solar system of Earth, where it spiraled in toward Elliott's part of the planet. Elliott was in a video arcade, throwing his last quarter to a machine on which he could never seem to score. He worked the joystick feverishly, missing every shot. E.T.'s telepathic wave came down, slightly off target, missing Elliott and landing in the back of the video machine. It perceived what Elliott wished, and began leaping around the circuits: Elliott's misfired salvos started scoring, one after another.

"Holy sh . . . !"

The machine shifted to a more difficult level, and Elliott kept scoring, game after game, as lights and super–sound effects started going off. "Highest score!" he shouted, blasting the last ship out of the screen.

In the midst of the electronic fireworks, fragments of invader ships arranged themselves into the shape of a pair of flickering letters—E T—but Elliott was too busy to notice. And in the next moment a certain girl passed through the video arcade.

"Hi, Elliott," she said, and Elliott felt a very odd sensation run through him, as if his knees had turned to soft ice cream and a bird had flown out of his heart.

He turned away from the machine, where E.T.'s message still flickered faintly, and he looked at— Julie. Her ponytail was tied with a little ring of rhinestones, which flickered in the light of the arcade.

He wanted to say something really cool and brilliant to her, maybe even remind her that he was the one who'd known the Extra-terrestrial. But he wasn't able to say anything cool or brilliant, because he'd just swallowed his gum while looking at her and it was lodged sideways in his throat. "Hi, Ju-lie," he croaked, but the noise of the arcade was so loud she seemed not to hear. Or maybe she heard and just pretended not to, which was a thing girls did. He was discovering that girls did *many* strange things, as strange and remote to Elliott as E.T. had been. "Girls are from another planet," he said to himself now, as he watched her walk on through the arcade.

He turned back to his game. And the message there, from another planet, had faded, and only ghostly spaceships moved back and forth across the screen.

*   *   *

E.T. sat in the botanical chamber, staring into Gertie's geranium. "This flower is Earth to me, and all happy memory."

His colleague, the other old botanist, looked up from his own work and walked over. He pointed a long finger into the petals of the geranium.

"It contains more than just Earth," he said, touching the grains of pollen. "These are traces of the sun."

He touched the carpel and the stamen. "This is a universal design."

He walked to the far wall and clicked a switch; a panel opened and a view screen appeared, out to the heavens. The Flower Nebula, pink-purple, floated before them, its great masses of gas and stardust in petal-like arrangements. "Your geranium comes from all that." He nodded to the great nebulous body before them. "Everything is connected in one great web. Is that not our first illumination?"

"Yes," said E.T., and his mind shifted into the higher range, as he remembered other times, places, initiations.

"You are an Adept in Cosmology," said his colleague. "You've been schooled in pure science. You're a learned being."

"True," said E.T. "How can I spend all day staring into a geranium? I have other responsibilities."

He gazed into the Flower Nebula. Within it was one of the greatest planets, whose appearance he could already discern—Mar'kinga Banda, giant planet, home of the super-strains of plantlife, whose trees towered into the clouds.

Its shape grew larger on the screen. "Yes, we're stopping there," said his colleague. "At Mar'kinga Banda, where the flowers are as big as this ship. You should prepare."

"Quite right," said E.T., suddenly excited again, his spirits lifting. "Mar'kinga Banda is a botanist's dream."

"The most exotic species imaginable."

"Plants whose intelligence is high and noble."

"Intellects towering as high as their own treetops."

"A planet of great truth and even greater beauty!"

E.T. opened his equipment chest, lifting out tubes, trays, slides, and his many cutting and digging tools. "...yes, yes..."

The ship was dropping quickly, already in the atmosphere of Mar'kinga Banda, the planet looming ever larger on the screen, the first details of its jungles appearing, bearing a roof of gigantic petals, from whose center sublime thought-waves beamed and sweet perfumes poured, strong enough to bring starships to narcosis and bend their trajectories to the land, for

Mar'kinga Banda wanted the pollen of the stars crossed with its own.

The ship sought its landing site and E.T. rushed with his colleague to the door leading from the Botanical Wing. His colleague stepped through, but when E.T. tried to follow, a Micro Tech intervened.

"Confined to quarters," smirked the superior little Tech, and began hooking up a weave of impassable light, bars of it, across the door.

E.T. gazed out through the bars, then turned and trudged back into the depths of the botanical chamber. He had a bunk on one of the flower tiers, and he climbed up into it now, and pulled the blanket over his head. Counting backward, he employed the hypnotic code and put himself into a deep sleep.

There he dreamed of the good times he'd had on Earth, living in a closet, eating candy, drinking beer, and wearing a wig. He saw Elliott and Michael, Mary, Gertie, and Harvey the dog, and he stayed asleep across the numberless eternities, dreaming of his friends as his ship went about its many missions and finally— returned home.

Home—causing all the heart-lights on shipboard to glow. The corridors were as if filled with roses, the color of love streaming everywhere. E.T. woke from his long dream, heart glowing up through his blanket, and suddenly it seemed to him as if Earth had been just that and only that—a dream—for here was his own world, calling to him and filling his heart. He threw off his blanket and went to the porthole. Yes, there it was—home, planet of many names, named by many ages—Vomestra, Brodo Asogi, Od-Di-Pa 5, Tum Lux O-ty, Alata Zerka, all of which translated to—the Green Planet. As Earth was called the Blue Planet for its waters, so E.T.'s home was called the Green Planet for its plant life, which flourished here as on no other planet in the world.

"Home, home, home." He paced about happily, chanting his favorite Earth word.

Other crew members looked in, heard him, and wondered what he was saying. Their word for home was *yammsoro*, meaning Exalted Organism, or more simply, One House For All. And the thought of it filled *them* with happiness.

But E.T. was no less happy, though he phrased his joy in an alien tongue. "Home, home, home." And he thought that maybe there'd even be a little band playing for him when he got off—for while he might be in the soup as far as the captain of the ship was concerned, the higher officials of the planet would certainly appreciate what he'd done—would recognize how important it was that he'd lived for weeks in a human closet.

"Home, home, home." He switched on the viewing screen, and there it was, floating below—the Green Planet, greater even than Mar'kinga Banda, for its plantlife was more evolved, husbanded over countless ages and bearing transplants from thousands of other planets. It was the great botanical garden of the cosmos, the breeding ground and storehouse for all known vegetal life. He himself had brought cuttings from far systems and planted them here, and tended them, in order to produce these immense gardens of loveliness, without equal in the world.

"Home, home, home." Plants of unparalleled powers and beauty—wise, sinister, flying, floating—masters of masquerade and allure, living embodiments of remote stellar forces, plants of mystery, plants untamed, plants of noble aspiration, godlike, immortal.

The ship swept downward. It would no doubt land in one of the great capital cities and there the high lords would greet him; there the beings of light, far older than he, would make a party in his honor, for his achievements on Earth. He'd give a lecture on Earth morphology, language, social structure and science, unveiling all his advanced mind had gathered and synthesized; also he'd show everyone how you had to have paper hats and whistles for a proper Earth party.

"Home, home, home." He saw a precious sight—the glow of one of the capitals, great Crystellum, whose gardens were perhaps the most beautiful of all. He'd certainly enjoy an assignment there, tending its decorative blossoms. The jeweled symmetrical splendor of Crystellum grew brighter, its supreme technology apparent everywhere, but bounded and interlaced with gardens of wonder. Yes, he'd be very happy working there, as befitted his rank, Doctor of Botany, First Class.

But the ship arced away from Crystellum, and sped on. Hapnod Illum, the second capital, appeared, but the ship also arced on over it, and it too fell behind. And then another and another, until the last great center, Lucidulum, was passed.

"They're taking you back," said the other old botanist, shuffling through the door.

"Back?"

"To the Farm."

The glow of Lucidulum faded, and the ship circled in over vast agricultural ranges, where the planet's food was grown. Here E.T. had worked the soil for hundreds of years, learning its secrets as a simple farmer. He began to recognize the terrain, from which he'd graduated long ago, after enormous struggle and very hard exams, following which he'd earned rank and joined a flight crew, and become a full-fledged intergalactical Doctor of Botany. And now—

"Demoted," said his colleague.

"To the bush league," said E.T., remembering how they would shout this on Earth TV each Saturn Day, when the man waving a stick too often missed the white sphere—*send him back to the bush league*. Also to be heard was the cry, *Send him to the showers!* He'd been sent to the showers on Earth, and it had almost killed him, lying there with Elliott, water running over him. That was when he'd been so sick, and he sincerely hoped he'd never be sent to the showers again.

"The ship sinks lower," said his colleague.

"My spirits sink with it."

Then a Micro Tech appeared at the door, and his thousand little fingers unhooked the electric bars. The signal for landing filled the ship, and a moment later it settled down, in the bush.

E.T. picked up his geranium, and his checker-board.

"Goodbye," said the other botanist.

E.T.'s heart began to glow with his own goodbye, to this colleague with whom he'd shared the millions of miles on the River of Stars, and who had been the only one in the troubled days of confinement to show E.T. special kindness. The glow in E.T.'s chest intensified, and a tiny core glowed most brightly, in the center of E.T.'s heart. It grew in intensity, then suddenly became an agitated whirl of light shaped like a jumping bean.

This bean contained the Tenth Symbol Code of the

Flower, a special field of inquiry E.T. alone had mastered, of all the botanical crew. It was concerned with the inner purpose of the Flower Soul, the part not seen by the eye, the ethereal portion—latent and hidden until flowering; this was the deepest of all botanical study, concerned with the archetypal forms of the Universal Seed, and E.T. was an Adept in it. His colleague was not, had studied other matters.

But the bean jumped, from E.T.'s heart into his colleague's. And all of E.T.'s work went with it, the whole of his study, all. It would have constituted an increase in rank for E.T., and honors, and more; but he gave it away now, to his colleague.

The other old botanist felt the bean of concentrated knowledge jump into his own heart, along an arc of light, which spread quite suddenly through his own body, and within moments he'd glimpsed and understood the spiritual significance of seed and chalice, of calyx, carpel, and corolla. He was dumbfounded at the gift, for a thousand years of work was in it, and more. Now it was his decoration, his wisdom, his honor, bestowed by a bean in a single flash. "Thank you, thank you," was all he could say, as tears of joy trickled down his cheeks, the great illumination flooding his nature. He turned toward the garden of the ship, a garden he now comprehended as never before. *So this,* he thought to himself, *is who my colleague has been.*

E.T., that colleague, now turned the other way, toward the door. He stepped into the corridor. It was empty, not even a Micro Tech around to wish him farewell. The outer hatch opened automatically, and he went down the gangplank, onto the soil of the Green Planet.

The starship closed up its gangplank, and he stared at it, confused, hardly able to believe that once more he was being left behind—and this time not by accident.

The ship lifted off, and he stepped backward, away from its radiance. At the porthole of the Botanical Wing, he saw a face—that of his colleague, waving sadly. E.T. waved back, his fingertip glowing with a feeble light.

And then the ship gained altitude, and withdrew, and he watched it go into the air and over the horizon, a last bit of light reflecting off its surface before it vanished.

He turned, disoriented. Which way was he to go? He began to walk, not caring where his footsteps took him. But before he'd gone far, a small local range cruiser came hurtling through the sky toward him. A moment later it was hovering before him, and the metallic petals of its hatchway opened. *"Enter,"* came the command from within.

He entered, and the petals immediately closed behind him. He was enclosed in a cubicle room. One of its walls opened, and a smaller cube rolled out on wheels; twin antennae emerged from its top surface, and a bank of lights flashed across its face. "Explain," said a mechanical voice from within it.

"I tried to b. good," said E.T.

"Not good enough." The interrogation machine wheeled around him, antennae quivering, as if examining him from all sides.

"I met the people of Earth," said E.T.

"We know. Please make your report." The voice of the machine was remote, superior, and E.T. knew it had been programmed by someone high in the planetary command. Would they try to confuse him, to be sure he wasn't making anything up? He looked down into his geranium and tried to collect his thoughts. Where could he possibly begin?

"Come, come," said the machine. "Describe their culture."

"They have an important celebration called Hollow Bean. Everyone carves faces in fruit squashes and dresses up in sheets. I myself dressed in one."

"Who holds this celebration?"

"The children, who actually rule the Blue Planet of Earth. They are much more intelligent and sensitive than the older people and outrun them on bicycles." E.T. nodded into his geranium. He was getting the facts straight, and the high command would learn much from his report, for inclusion in the Galactical Encyclopedia.

The machine circled around him again. "And what is the purpose of this celebration?"

"To collect the all-important food, which is candy."

"Candy?"

"D. licious," said E.T.

The machine paused, an odd buzzing sound coming from inside it, as if it was having difficulty assimilating information. Finally, its voice resumed: "Did you meet the ruler of Earth?"

"Elliott."

"Elliott is the ruler? How old is he? Has he ten-thousand years?"

"He's ten."

"Ten? And he rules?"

"With his brother Michael who is also called Penis Breath."

The machine's lights blinked violently, and this was followed by more static buzzing. Then: "And did this Earth ruler, Elliott, and his associate Penis Breath, treat you with respect? Did they acknowledge the advanced nature of your intellect?"

"They kept me in what is called a closet, where the most prized possessions are kept, among them Kermit the Frog, and a collection of illustrated works on the life of the great Flash Gourd On."

E.T. began to breathe more easily. The interview was going well, without confusion.

"And what form of enlightenment did you give these young rulers?"

"We drank beer and stole things. The police chased us and many objects in our way got creamed."

"Creamed?"

"A special Earth word," said E.T., in his rough, gravelly voice. "I know many such now."

The machine buzzed with confusion again, rolled forward, then backward, then bumped into a wall. It rotated slowly toward him. "Depart."

The hatchway opened and E.T. shuffled back out, holding his geranium. He felt the debriefing had been very successful and now that they saw how much valuable information about Earth he'd brought, they'd call him back up from the league of bushes.

The petal hatchway of the cruiser closed, and the vessel rose up, and sped away, leaving him deep in the outer agricultural ranges, alone, to figure things out, which he did, immediately.

"Creamed," he said to himself, and began to walk along, toward the old Farm.

* * *

The path ran over hills and through forests. The trees were mostly Jumpums, of great vigor, having evolved from a time of terrible drought on the Green Planet, when their desperate search for water had caused them to lift themselves out of the soil, roots and all, and move on; the movement had evolved through the ages until now the entire family of Jumpum trees took short hops every so often, and then dug their roots like frenzied claws deep into the soil. This meant that no path in a Jumpum forest was ever in one place for very long, for Jumpums could obliterate it in a minute or so, and frequently did, jumping all over it.

E.T. opened his mental band into the telepathic mode, to help him find his way to friendly and familiar surroundings; he was tracking with some success, though a bunch of Jumpums jumping all around you, if you're not used to them, can be upsetting, and he scolded a few of them for jumping almost on top of him, their roots pinning his long toes in place. "B. good."

They looked at him sadly, their leaves drooping to the ground as they backed off, for he was a distinguished botanist and they were just silly young Jumpums.

"I'm sorry," he said, and jumped around with them for a while to make them feel better; his short legs did not get him far in the jumping category but the Jumpums didn't care, and jumped merrily. He left them as they started to organize a jumping contest, which was much too strenuous for anyone but a Jumpum. He walked on, carrying his geranium.

The colors of the day—rich gold and red in the clouds—showed that afternoon was ending. Shadows began to fall in the forest as he walked. A stream of water, deep purple in hue, flowed beside him, and ancient lizards basked on its banks.

E.T.'s brain, in rapport with the lizards, picked up their dark reflections, mostly magical and coldly calculating, but the lizards had many sound ideas and were revered for their philosophical insight. Listening to them as he walked, E.T.'s mind, an extraterrestrial organ quite unlike anything on Earth, resumed its old perceptions. He began to think once again in terms of millennia, rather than months or years; again he felt the slow pulse of the unfolding universal ages, mastery of which was the birthright of the Green Planet. His cosmic memory, recently suppressed, flowered again and he was once more able to effortlessly contemplate things in the whole—the universe as entity, all parts related.

Beneath his feet silvery mosses yielded, leaving luminescent threads upon his toes; feathery fronds hanging low brushed his brow, reminding him of all he'd so recently forgotten—that home was a world of mental delicacies, where the solar mind had strongly focused, supported by twin moons, one near and one far, to produce cosmic thinkers, Mind Holders, as the elite of the flight crews were called. He was a candidate for such honors, of great mental transcendence, somewhere distant in time. As a child of the Green Planet, he was heir to that.

"Home," he said to himself once again, as he stepped through a pool of liquid jade, fed by nephrite streams, cool and gleaming; it flowed around his ankles and rippled past, whispering its own secret of antiquity here, on the planet of paradise. He waded slowly out, absorbing the forgotten dream. All this was his, forever.

His telepathic receiver suddenly produced an image of someone ahead, of his own intelligence. He was approaching the edge of the great agricultural domain. A few more steps brought him out of the forest, and into a field. In it a solitary figure worked, bent over a long cultivated row. He looked much like E.T. but his neck did not seem able to raise itself as high.

"A youngster," said E.T. to himself. "Only several hundred years old. Doing the work I once did."

The youthful creature was tending a crop of legumes called Igios Atra, or as they were more affectionately known—Beeperbeans, which gave off a sharp beeping sound when their blossoms opened. As it was springtime, there was considerable beeping going on, and the worker had corks in his ears.

I'll just give him a little surprise...

E.T. was beside the youngster before he knew it, and when the little fellow turned, a cry sprang from his lips and the corks popped out of his ears.

"Excuse me, Doctor," he said, addressing E.T. by his proper title. "I didn't know—*beep*—you were—*beep beep*—making your rounds—*beep.*"

"Proceed," said E.T., not wanting to admit to this mere child that he'd soon be tending Beeperbeans himself, and hear beeps in his sleep, and talk in beeps, and nearly be a beep, before spring was complete.

But then he paused, and said to the youngster, "Let me show you a trick with the Beeperbean, one that will reduce your discomfort. The Beeperbean, you see, can be influenced so as to confine its beeping to early morning only. I discovered this quite by accident—" And shall have to make use of it myself once again, he added to himself, as he took the youngster to the nearby wood and pointed out an herb called

Noorf-og-inki, or Essence of Pure Silence. "Nothing can completely subdue a Beeperbean, of course, for they are so exuberant, but a few pinches of this in the nutrient flow will save your eardrums."

"My deep-beep-est gratitude, Doctor," said the student botanist. "It will save my eardrums and ... beep beep ... my sanity ... beep. For I confess to beep-being half-crazed and beep-becoming worse every hour."

"Yes, well, I also suggest ... beep ... suggest you discard the corks from your ears and use beep-beeswax instead. It's much beep-beep-better."

"Thank you, Doctor, for beep-befriending."

"Not at all. But now I must beep-be leaving you. So, b.beep good."

The youngster began preparing the Essence of Pure Silence for the nutrient bath, and E.T. strolled the length of the row, and the next, and then crossed a little footbridge over the irrigation canal, where blue fluid waited to be cycled through the entire root system of the field. Stepping from the bridge, he entered a grove of Fluteroots, which were grown near Beeperbeans to provide psychological relief from the incessant beeping. The Fluteroots swayed in the breeze, and the breeze moved through their hollow stalks, playing melodies of delicate beauty.

"The charm of the Fluteroots is good," said E.T., addressing them respectfully in the language of plants, which he, as a master botanist knew in all its varying shades. He closed his eyes and swayed with the plants, as their pure flowing sound moved all through him.

"Memories of my youth are returning to me," he said with a sigh, and the Fluteroots tooted sweetly in response. Longer shadows of evening fell in the grove, and still he swayed, forgetful of time and season, and of his recent demotion and disgrace. But as the giant sun set, turning the sky to bronze, he woke, and remembered.

"Let me go now," he said, and the Fluteroots played more softly, releasing him from their spell. He left the grove, and entered the next field, and the next, going through the rows as of old, when at sunset one would look upon the work and be glad, and amazed, by the perfect symmetry of it. Except for the excessive beeping, it was a most satisfying place.

He climbed a gentle slope, whose face was covered with more luminous moss, a cultivated crop with a mixture of many colors, rainbow-like and almost as mysterious, the little mosses under the ministrations of the moons, whose soft glow they had absorbed and which robed them now. He crested the hill and a vast patchwork of fields appeared before him in the reddish bronze of evening.

"Nowhere in the countless worlds are there such gardens as these," he said aloud, "gardens whose purity and power sustain an immortal race."

The squares below him, where the plants were now folding inward toward rest, were the result of cultivation spanning eons; the locks of longevity had been opened, by keys the plants themselves had provided. "—for you are wise," said E.T., "in your quiet way, far wiser than the restless creatures who feed upon you in this world."

He crossed the spine of the hill, and saw another familiar sight—one of the pocket villages used by the workers who attended the surrounding fields.

The village, like the fields, was an organic thing, a hybrid—for the cottages of the agriculturalists had not been built, but grown. A little biochemistry and some saturated nutrients had produced a species of gourd called Chemon Xrus, meaning Big Enough To Live In. Such a gourd was four-chambered, waterproof, and sweet-smelling. Once dried, it was hard as a super alloy, and yet always gave the feeling of being enclosed in an entity connected to the force of nature, a most secure and comfortable aspect, conducive to advanced introspection.

E.T. hurried down the slope toward the ring of giant gourds. Herb gardens surrounded them, lined with huge rough crystals, by which the herbs were stimulated, the crystals glittering in the red glow of evening, drawing in the concentrated solar force, their clear latticed interiors shot with streaks of red. Villages like this were found everywhere in the agricultural province, but this particular one was special to E.T.

He hurried through the herbal ring, along a green gravel path, his heart-light glowing. From one of the gourds, an answering light came from a window, which grew rose-bright, so bright the light splashed down the wrinkled sides of the gourd, and onto E.T.'s own wrinkled face. Panting, racing, he ran up the path to the gourd, the door of which was now glowing all around the edges.

It swung open before E.T., and he entered.

Standing within was a creature like E.T., but tall and stately, having entered the late second growth stage, in which the mental stature produces a sudden acceleration of the physique, resulting in such an elegantly slender being as now stood before E.T. The creature's heart-light was brilliant, ablaze with solar wisdom.

"Parent," said E.T. softly, and approached with hesitant step.

The glow of their natures merged, ruby light filling the cottage. E.T. closed his eyes and felt the ineffable flowing of the ancestral force—a parade appearing in his mind, in which thousands moved, including those most early forebears, the Magicians, whose practice in nature had produced the race of scientists to which he himself belonged.

As he was contemplating all this, and feeling the arc of the ages, the voice of the Parent spoke above him in the ancient and exalted language of the planet, softly rasping and so expressive. "Well, child, you certainly made a mess of things."

E.T. opened his eyes. The great Parent was sighing, with a slow shake of its noble head; but then a long arm reached out and embraced E.T. Hearts merged still more deeply, saying things for which there are no words; this Parent, sole creator of E.T.'s form out of its own nature, was both father and mother to him, and E.T. was bathed in the healing force of this, and in its stern judgment.

"Come, let us talk."

He was led into that chamber of the gourd used for visits. It was furnished with objects that, like the gourd, had been biochemically engineered—a couch of velvety texture, made of mosses grown upon a shelf of the gourd's own sculpted interior; a chair of the same soft design; and a deliberately stunted table-tree, gnarled roots embedded in the floor, upper surface a fine mesh of tightly woven leaves. Pitcher plant blossoms, lacquered and polished, served as cups and bowls.

E.T. set his geranium on the table, in the soft light of the visiting chamber.

"That is a most beautiful plant," said the Parent, and just the sound of the Parent's subtly modulated voice and the attention of its sensitive gaze, caused the little geranium to stir, and the flush of its petals deepened in the richness of their color.

The chamber was lit by Lumens, a species of large phosphorescent grub, perfectly domesticated, which clung to the walls of the gourd and dined on minute organisms living there, which made it convenient for all concerned, as the organisms were happier within the grubs, attending to the grub's digestion and producing light thereby. Five or six Lumens gave quite enough light to read by, a nice even glow falling all around.

"So," said the Parent, when they were seated facing each other in the chamber, "what exactly did you do on Earth?"

"Peeked in windows."

"Peeked in windows? You? A Botanist of the Capital, First Class?"

E.T. swung his feet back and forth nervously. Now was the time for an eloquent explanation, drawing upon his full powers. "I felt a compelling scientific need to study the alien habitat more closely—to observe the hominid beings within their social sphere—"

The Parent frowned, a frown that meant, speak more clearly.

"I goofed," said E.T. "The quick tongue of Earth tells it better."

"And now what?"

"Farmed out."

They sat in silence then, as night fell. In the soft glow of the Lumens, E.T. studied the Parent's face, whose eyes were deep with manifold insights gained over immensities of time. All experience seemed to reside there, with the possible exception of peeking in windows, which distinction, thought E.T., is reserved for me.

"In all the history of the planet there is no one who has goofed as badly as I have."

"You always were too curious," said the Parent.

"True, too true."

The Parent sighed again. "You traveled from one end of the universe to the other, you saw a thousand worlds, worlds few creatures are privileged to see— great, unexplainable systems of astounding beauty, teeming with amazing sights to behold—and you had to go peek in a window."

E.T. put his head in his hands. He had no excuse. He'd made a mess of his career, had disgraced the Parent, and was in deep soup all around.

Later, when all was quiet in the gourd, and the Parent was sleeping, E.T. went out into the forest and picked those night-blooming herbs that he alone knew how to combine—into a scent that would soothe a troubled mind. It was an herbal packet only masters of botany could manage, for the moment of picking was crucial and the moons were involved. He labored all night, through the shadows of the forest, from glade to glade, until he had the packet he wanted, one whose special powers of tranquility were unsurpassed.

"A very strong packet is required," he reminded himself, and added yet a few more ingredients, so that he had the very quintessence of that which is soothing, which erases recent disagreeable incident, and neutralizes disappointment. A sachet of this sort, left within a sleeper's room, would rearrange the elements in the mind into higher patterns, so that what seemed at first to be discord would be seen as a secret sort of harmony.

"At least I hope so," he said to himself, and returned to the gourd. He crept to the Parent's bedside, where he placed the soothing packet of herb magic on the pillow beside the Parent's head.

"Do your work," he whispered to the sachet, *"for my dear progenitor has had a lot to put up with of late, as regards a certain member of the family."*

E.T. watched for a moment, and when he saw a frown line soften on the Parent's head, and a troubled pressure around the eyes release, he knew he had succeeded. And he crept from the room as if he were the spirit of the herb called Silence.

He's back, he's back!

This one thought was racing through the head of a creature known scientifically as the Igigi Gyrum Hadahadeba, meaning Six-hundred Vertebrae In The Spine. But everyone on the Green Planet just called them Flopglopples, for one of their modes of travel was to flop around like a long gloppy length of something, with a tripodial arrangement of feet at the bottom. Of all things, they perhaps resembled most closely a pile of gray floppy socks. They were very fast, very agile, very stupid, and very loving. And this particular one was devoted to E.T.

"Back, he's back in our system of reference so we can now say he is here now whereas before we couldn't say he was anywhere now because he was thirty-eight light-years away quite beyond the now."

There are some Green Planet scientists who say that Flopglopples are old and very wise. However, this has never been proven, as Flopglopples enjoy giving silly answers on intelligence tests.

In any case, the Flopglopple was hurrying along, flopping in sidewinder fashion, so fast that little but dust could be seen—sailing over the hilltop and flopping down the other side of it, toward the agricultural village.

"He's been gone such a long time but time is an impalpable thing. And I'm rushing along though it is futile to speak of the motion of a single body."

Thus, the Flopglopple.

A moment more and he was speeding through the village, green gravel flying out from underneath his tripod of flopping feet. He raced past the sign saying *Flopglopples Slow Down,* and sent gravel up against a number of window panes.

He skidded to a stop in front of E.T.'s cottage, ran around it excitedly, and finally flopped in over a windowsill, as it was open and the door was not, and Flopglopples believe in expediency. A millisecond later he was flopped around E.T.'s shoulders, draped like a stole and hugging him devotedly.

"B. good," said E.T., as the Flopglopple hung upside down, looking him in the eyes with a smile.

"Let us dine," said the Parent, and poured from the pitcher plant beaker, into the blossom cups. The liquid was ambrosial, with all needed nutrients, and was served with biscuits similarly constituted, but E.T. could not help thinking the repast was not in the same class as a handful of Reese's Pieces and a bottle of beer. However, he thanked the Parent, gave some ambrosia and biscuit to the Flopglopple, and sat back on the couch, gazing out at the lighted village. In many ways, it beat living in a closet. But still, there was a tug within him.

El-li-ott, he said softly to himself, and a telepathic wave went out from between his brows, pierced the roof of the gourd, and then streaked on its way.

He'd taken the obligatory navigational courses for telepathic senders, but had cut most of the classes in order to continue his more interesting botanical researches, and go swimming in the nephrite streams. Therefore, his thought-wave entered the space-time vector two degrees off course, the result being his little telepathic replicant arrived on Earth in the middle of a shopping mall, specifically on the fast food counter, and the tiny telepathic replicant, in every way resembling E.T., landed in the mustard bowl. He climbed out, and was struck by a plastic tray, which knocked him down the counter into the cash register. It opened with a bang behind him and sent him flying into the ice cream blender.

As he was whirling around in the cream, the little tele-replicant got the feeling that someone he knew was near.

In fact, Elliott's mother, Mary, was seated at the counter on her lunch hour, wondering: "Why am I about to eat a hamburger, two hot dogs, a double order of french fries, a milk shake, and a cupcake covered with dyed candy sprinkles?"

It's part of the Doctor Debauchee Eat-everything-you-possibly-can Diet, she reflected. Tomorrow I'll take up speed walking.

"Here you go, ma'am," said the counterboy, handing her the gross offering.

"Thank you so much," said Mary, staring at what she'd ordered. She'd have to eat it as quickly as she could before anyone recognized her.

She carried the tray to one of the tables set up in the central hallway of the mall, which gave her the pleasant feeling of eating in the lobby of an insane asylum.

"Lunch hour is so important for the working woman," she said to herself as she lifted her hot dog, "especially when shared with someone magnetic and interesting." The mall janitor, whose stomach might benefit from a forklift to carry it, began emptying the adjacent trash basket.

His arm, observed Mary, is covered with scrambled egg. Now he's getting some ketchup on his elbow. He's hard-working but what would we talk about in the evenings?

She set down her hot dog and picked up her hamburger. No, I need someone more sensitive, who can say things with his eyes.

She looked into her milk shake and saw, fleetingly, a little wrinkled being, floating in the foam.

I'm hallucinating.

What did they *put* in this relish? She looked at the trailing edge of her hamburger.

Then she looked down at her cupcake, where the tiny candy sprinkles were arranging themselves and spelling M A R Y.

I'm simply undergoing computer shock, too many hours in the typing pool, watching little letters dance around on the green screen.

She tapped the janitor on the back. "Sir, would you please tell me what's written on this cupcake?" She held it up to him.

"You've been shoppin' too long, lady. I seen it before. Go home, relax." He moved on to the next trash can.

She stared after him. He's *awfully* nice. But would we find the weekends too long?

She laid the cupcake back on her tray, upside-down. Whatever it said, it was only another sign of the divorced, early middle-aged woman wishing for a call from someone. Even a cupcake.

She turned and saw Elliott coming down the hall-way of the mall. How unfortunate that he was going to see his own mother stuffing herself with the very foods she tried to pretend she never ate. Oh well, that was the mother business—to be always caught off-guard, humiliated, and finally disgraced.

"Hi, Mom," he said. "Pigging out?"

"Yes, dear."

"Mom, did you see any friends of mine around? I just had the funniest feeling that somebody I knew was here."

"Sorry, Elliott, I haven't seen anyone."

"I keep having the feeling I told someone I'd meet them here at the fast food place."

"Well, did you?"

"No." He looked at her cupcake. "I'd better help you out, Mom," he said, and grabbed it from her plate. She thought of grabbing it back but decided a mother should not be seen fighting with her son over pastry in a public place. And in any case, Elliott didn't even give her the chance. He was already moving off down the hallway of the mall, following a pretty little girl with a rhinestoned ponytail.

"Y ou should report to the fields," said the Parent.

E.T. nodded. It was morning in the gourd and he was an agriculturalist once more. The faithful Flop-glopple went out of his gourd with him, onto the gravel path. The great solar body hung before them, and the dawn sky was copper, metallically brilliant streaks of light pouring through atmospheric veils of neon, argon, and zyonidon.

"This way," said E.T., taking a back path. "I don't want to meet anyone."

"Why not?"

"Because I'm in disgrace."

"Oh, that's nothing," said the Flopglopple. "I'm

always in disgrace for racing through villages and otherwise acting up."

"It's nothing for you, because it is your nature," said E.T. "But I'm a scholar, a scientist."

"And I am like light," said the Flopglopple, zigging back and forth on the path. "I cannot be brought to rest. At birth I begin accelerating and steadily increase my velocity!"

The Flopglopple gave a display of his swiftness and dexterity, weaving in and out of the trees in a blur, and E.T. suddenly recalled how he himself had flown on Earth. At first, when everyone was chasing him, he hadn't known he could do it, but then suddenly he'd discovered the thing. "Wouldn't it be wonderful if I surprised the Flopglopple and flew right over him?"

He lifted one leg, bent it back, took a flying leap, and sank down in a heap some 25 centimeters away. Jumpum trees all around him bounced out, clapping their branches and lifting him up.

Try again! they said, for they loved leaps and bounces of any kind.

"No, no, that's all the bouncing for now." He fended them off and continued along the shaded morning path, toward the fields. The Flopglopple was ahead, teasing the ancient lizards of the forest, who looked at him with slitted eyes, and then looked at E.T., tongues flickering in a whisper.

Get this Igigi Gyrum out of here.

E.T. attempted to restrain the Flopglopple. "Never tease lizards."

"They're so stiff and scaly," said the Flopglopple. "I can't help myself." He tweaked the distinguished reptiles by the tails.

Vestigial idiot, grumbled the lizards.

The Flopglopple turned to E.T. "Don't listen to them. I will prove useful. Through the mask of my clowning, some see my virtues."

Atrophied imbecile, muttered the lizards, and slithered off into the leaves.

"I'm older than they are," said the Flopglopple, winding himself around a tree trunk like a python. "I've gone back to the sea and emerged again. And someday I'll grow wings."

Someday, said a scaly voice from within the leaves, *you'll grow a rudimentary brain.*

"I'll run ahead," said the Flopglopple, "and see what's there!" Saying which, he vanished in a whirl of leaves and dust. E.T. followed, to the forest's edge. Before him were the fields, stretching to the horizon. From them, morning vapors arose, and through the mist that hugged the rows he saw the agriculturalists moving—creatures like himself, but all young, much younger, their knowledge just beginning to form.

"While mine is complete. A complete fool."

But thoughts of his folly on Earth made him long for his friend there, and a tele-beam went out from his forehead and headed for Earth. Through star systems and dimension gates it traveled, and the little tele-replicant of E.T. came down, almost on target, in Elliott's classroom.

It was a computer class, and the little replicant landed in Elliott's machine. Seeing a good opportunity at hand, the tele-replicant began creating a message from within the computer. A single word, telling all, flashed on Elliott's screen:

Owch

But Elliott was looking across the aisle at a certain young lady he'd grown strangely attracted to lately—for Elliott had grown in years since the time E.T. had left. Time-travel distorts and while E.T. had aged little, Elliott had grown and entered junior high school—and found new interests there.

Such as this girl, whose long ponytail fascinated him in ways he could not quite explain.

Owch Owch Owch

said the screen. But Elliott's head was still turned.

"All right, class," said the teacher. "Clear your machines."

Elliott, still looking at the young lady, pressed a single button, and E.T. was wiped out of memory.

* * *

E.T. stood at the edge of the agricultural fields. The young workers there drew back deferentially as he approached, for they could feel his higher mind, and they could see for themselves how the plants were responding to E.T.'s presence—buds opening as if to greet him.

"Kish mitobit eront hoyat nurabong . . ." He walked through the plants, murmuring softly to them in their own tongue, and touching them with his healing, glowing index finger—the mark of a Botanist First Class, even a demoted one. The plants responded, the long row unfolding its tiny leaves as he passed, and the agricultural students looked on, dreaming of the day when they too could make a plant respond in such arcane ways.

Then E.T. himself felt a higher wave, far higher than his own, an emanation partaking directly of the solar and lunar forces, the wave length of his teacher—Botanicus.

It spread through the field, touching all the growing things, a power like E.T.'s, but amplified many times, the radiance of an Adept in Agriculture. There were only a few such on the planet, and of them Botanicus was the greatest. His glittering thought-wave, like a stream of diamonds, broke along the row, dazzling all who stood there, and dazzling still more those rooted there.

Following in the wake of this powerful thought-wave, Botanicus appeared. His form was like the Parent—tall and slender, of the advanced growth cycle. He was wrapped in a robe made of a large leaf, whose tips were tucked around his shoulders and under his arms. It clung to him, undying, sustained by his emanation. His walk was slow and stately, and a large jade-skinned lizard accompanied him, forked tongue flickering as he waddled along beside his master.

Botanicus gestured to the plants, all ten of his fingertips glowing with the marks of the Adept.

"Each shining fingertip," said E.T. softly to the students, "represents an achievement of wisdom so great that it glows, and is with him always, as a power at his command."

As Botanicus gestured, as the light streamed from his fingers, new shoots appeared all along the row, buds multiplied, and leaves that had been scarred by insects were healed.

A sigh went through the young students, and E.T. himself was filled with awe, as always. These fields, as far as the eye could see and farther, belonged to Botanicus. The food supply of half the planet was under his care; these were his gardens, and here he had dwelled and worked through the eons.

"Here," said E.T. to the students, "Botanicus solved the riddle of life; here he learned the innermost secrets of all that grows, above and below."

Around Botanicus was a corona of shimmering light, and plants swooned as he passed, some falling, some rising, some reaching out to touch him and draw more of his concentrate. Where his footsteps fell, seedlings suddenly sprouted, quickened by his impress, and where his gaze landed, there a plant would tremble with rapture. Most learned, Supreme Scientist, Lord of the Fields—Botanicus.

He seemed not to see his pupils yet, his gaze only for the plants, and E.T. and the young workers simply followed him through the row, E.T. remembering again that the secret of life was an equation of love, inexpressibly tender and haunting. Botanicus, great Botanicus, had solved that equation to its depth, down the spiraling helix. Thousands of new plant forms were his creation, and through them he fed the planet— no one hungry, all sustained and nourished by his vision.

Finally he turned, his gaze now falling on his students, and then on E.T. His large limpid eyes blinked slowly. "Prize pupil." He extended his hand to E.T. "Come here, pride and joy."

E.T. moved in front of him. Botanicus put his leathery palm on E.T.'s head and closed his eyes. "Rhizome blocked. Sap down in the toes. What's wrong?"

"Weeded out," said E.T. "Kicked off the ship."

"Unfortunate," said Botanicus. His gaze remained gentle. "But you have been returned to me, and I cannot say I'm sorry about that. Yes, Doctor, I foresee that we shall make some new breakthrough together."

The eyes of Botanicus shone with clairvoyant brightness. His lizard whipped its tail once, back and forth, and its eyes became narrowed slits, as perhaps it too contemplated the faint shadows of E.T.'s future. And on both sides, the other students of Botanicus, still bearing the fuzz of immaturity on their heads, looked on spellbound. But their hair moss glowed amber and silver, as if filling with some premonition of a strange and powerful event on the horizon.

"Come," said Botanicus, and gestured for them to follow him, deeper into the fields. The gardens of Botanicus were vast, and many thousands worked for him, near and far. E.T. felt the teacher's ray stream out to the plants, and down into the nuclei of their cells.

"We can affect them," said Botanicus, stroking a green leaf. "We can touch their nucleotide sequence, the acids, the enzymes, the proteins, and cause them to alter, as we desire."

And so the gardens of Botanicus contained many bizarre creations, the most unusual of which, perhaps, was the agi Jabi. One of them stood at the end of the row, a tall plant, something like corn, but which had been crossed with a Jumpum and Shrieking Ja—to produce a plant who guarded the field from marauding birds. If birds came by, the agi Jabi leapt out, waved its stalks and produced a deafening cry, after which it would go back to its silent vigil. Like most hybrids, it was temperamental and shrieked at everyone who came along—except for Botanicus, whom it recognized and loved.

"My good agi Jabi," said Botanicus, petting it. "The fields are under your care."

A budlike protuberance at the top of the stalk turned, and a fibrous lid lifted, revealing a collection of yellow crystals, which were agi Jabi's sly and crafty eye. E.T. stepped carefully around the plant, as did the other students, for the cry of agi Jabi was nerve-shattering at best. Botanicus whispered to it, and it allowed the class to pass by.

Ahead were rows of beaker plants—each blossom a large transparent globe in which methane, ammonia, and hydrogen sulphide floated.

"Each a potential world," said Botanicus. He gestured over the plants, and the gases stirred. "The beginning of things," he said, and looked at the agriculturalists, and at E.T., the strange clairvoyant gleam in his eyes once again. "Create what you desire. The elements are here—" He pointed again at the beaker plants. "The power is *there*—" He pointed at a row of little plants, whose solid round buds were expanding and contracting, making carbohydrates and burning them with a rumbling noise.

So the morning passed, as they tended the rows, and then, when it was time for a rest, they followed Botanicus into a grove of Fluteroots, where the music of the wind played softly, and everyone gathered around the teacher.

"One must be careful in one's experiments," he said. "Once, accidentally, I used too much elixir of Antum Tadana, whose power to strengthen fiber you all know. As a result, I created a plant with roots like the hardest alloy of metals. These vigorous, indestructible roots began to sink themselves ever more deeply into the ground." He paused and looked at the group, and his eyes sparkled. "It pierced the planet's crust, penetrating the sila and the sima, and began digging its way through the mantle. It pierced the asthenosphere and found what it was seeking—the fiery magma at the planetary core, for it was a plant of volcanic inclinations. It sucked the magma up its shoot and its blossoms were turned into flame and lava, which it spewed forth for miles. Dangerous, indeed, was that plant."

Botanicus looked at E.T. and smiled. "I have the feeling that the powers of Antum Tadana will draw you, as they once drew me."

E.T. nodded, and decided it was his cue to tell a story of his own, of Earth, to give the students further information that might one day prove useful to them.

"Earth has many strange creatures," he began. "Most strange are some I lived with. They sit on shelves and never move, though they have arms and legs, and they never eat though they have mouths, they are called *toys* and have definite spiritual qualities and indeed frequently spoke to me in the silence of the closet. I believe them to be very advanced, as are our great meditative sages, the Mind Holders." He paused, to gather more profundities for his young listeners, whose head-moss was again beginning to glow amber and silver, as they leaned toward him.

"I shared my quarters with another remarkable creature called the Baa Sket Ba, who is a little round being filled with air, much like our beaker blossoms.

He is helpless to go anywhere unless you bounce him. Earth people love him and try to take him from each other every Saturn Day. I saw this on their communication screen, before which I sat drinking beer as all Earth people do and I felt wonderful but later had a mysterious pain in my head."

The young workers' mouths had fallen open. E.T. nodded wisely, happy to be educating them to the way of worlds far from home, which they themselves might one day visit, and for which they should have the correct preparation.

"There," said Botanicus to his pupils. "Now you know something of Earth." He looked again at E.T., and one eye opened slightly wider, brow lifting quizzically.

E.T. raised his healing finger, in which many powers were contained. He must give something to Botanicus, whom he'd not seen in so long and to whom he owed so much. And though his teacher was far wiser than he, and counted all the treasures of botany as his own, there was one thing E.T. could give, the gift which an Adept can give to an Elder, even though the Elder knows much more than the Adept. Botanicus saw E.T.'s gesture beginning and shook his head. "Do not shorten your own cycle."

But the gift of the life-force was already leaping, from the core of E.T.'s being, from the store of his life-potential. He was giving a cycle of his own life, consisting of an entire century, to Botanicus. His healing finger glowed, and the light leapt into Botanicus, at the point called Energic Door, in the top of the skull.

The gathered students drew their breath in awe, for they had never seen this gift before. And a moment later they saw its manifestation; an age ring had vanished from the dome of Botanicus's head, where the cycles were counted as in the trunk of a tree. He had regained the form he'd held a hundred years ago, and a new vigor was in his gaze as he once more raised his head.

"A fine gift, Doctor," he said softly, and cast his eyes to E.T.'s own brow, where the vanished ring had formed, E.T. having gathered Botanicus's weariness to himself. E.T. turned away then, as if nothing had passed, and gazed into the fields which he and Botanicus served. He felt the heaviness of a full cycle upon him but he would carry it for Botanicus; it was only right that he do so.

* * *

E.T. worked all day beside the others, at jobs he hadn't done for ages. His Flopglopple, after running amok in the rows for several hours, settled down beside him to help with the soil test. The Flopglopple was an excellent gardener, spoke the language of plants and was most gentle in transplanting. "We're back on the job," he said to E.T. affectionately.

"Yes," said E.T., "it is pleasant work." But his head kept turning skyward, sunward and beyond, and a mental wave went out, entered the wormholes of space, jumped universes, and found Earth.

It orbited, and began final descent, coming down in a row of phone booths near the school bus stop, where Elliott and his friends had gathered. E.T.'s telereplicant got twisted up in the telephone currents, its message spiraling out and into the ear of a salesman using the phone. "Forty-two pairs of bikini briefs, size medium, yessir, I'll be delivering them this afternoon." He hung up, and for no reason he could think of, phoned home.

"Hello, Mother, this is Sheldon...no I'm not in jail. Mother, please, I don't need a loan, I'm selling underwear. Mother, would you spare me your sarcasm? Does Dad need any boxer shorts? No, that's not why I'm calling, I don't *know* why I'm calling, I suddenly had this urge to *phone home."*

Elliott climbed into the school bus and it moved off down the block.

He walked down the aisle of the bus, behind his friends. He'd sit with them and pretend he hadn't noticed Julie get on. When dealing with girls you had to pretend right back—that you didn't care about them, that you'd rather be punching a friend, or shouting hysterically. That was the way it was done; that was the only way to get someplace with girls—to go no place at all.

He couldn't help wondering if there wasn't something basically incorrect about the procedure.

"Hey, Elliott, did you see the latest *Heavy Metal?"*

The magazine made the rounds, and he pretended to peruse it, but the words and pictures weren't making any sense, for he'd just heard Julie whispering his name to the girl beside her, two seats away in the bus. Were they talking about how cool and detached he was?

Could they see that he was trying to grow some very sharp sideburns, which at the moment looked something like a weasel's tail?

He turned toward them, as if looking out the other side of the bus at something very interesting there, even though the bus was going through an underpass and nothing was visible but pigeon-spattered bricks.

He gazed at the pigeon-spatter thoughtfully, in a scientific manner. Maybe Julie would think he was making an important study. "Very interesting," he muttered softly. His friend Greg spoiled the tableau by hitting him on the head with a rolled up *Rolling Stone*.

"Hey, Elliott, wake up! Who are you lookin' at— Julie? Hey, Julie—" Greg turned to her. "Elliott's got it bad for you!"

"Creep!" retorted Elliott, giving Greg a sharp jab on the arm. But everybody in the bus was laughing, a crazed kind of laughter that swept through them like a wind, blowing their emotions about. But Elliott felt the wind's secret meaning, beyond the laughs and cackles of his idiot friends. His eyes met Julie's and he felt a terribly familiar feeling, and yet where had he ever had such a feeling before? Her eyes were soft and inviting, and he'd never seen *that* before. And yet it was so familiar, as if he'd known it always. Oh no, he moaned inside himself, this is what life is all about.

A tortured joy ran through him, and he had to look away, from those long lashes softly blinking.

* * *

A universe away, E.T. turned to the Flopglopple. "My aim is off."

The Flopglopple twisted his noodley fingers into something resembling a scope-sight and held it in the air. "Aim your mental wave through here."

"Don't be silly."

"Very well," said the Flopglopple, and unfolded his fingers, with some difficulty.

They were alone in their row, but there was a sudden shivering in the air. The Flopglopple looked up and craned his limber neck. "Ios Naba coming."

The Ios Naba, or Contentment Monitor, was streaking along over the fields, from row to row. It zipped into E.T.'s row—a whirlpool of multicolored light whose center resembled an eye.

The Monitor, whose job was to see that everyone was happy, whirled up to the Flopglopple. A lens-like flutter appeared in the center of its whirling pool of light, out of which a thin voice emerged. "You're doing fine, much happier today," it said to the Flop-glopple, who smiled and pointed at E.T.

"The doctor is back."

"I see, I see," said the Contentment Monitor, and it expanded its whirling pool of color until it had enveloped E.T., feeling every nuance of his mood. "Something's wrong. Can't have that. Tell your Con-tentment Monitor all about it. You'll feel much bet-ter."

"I miss my friend."

"Fine, I'll get him." The Contentment Monitor pointed itself. "Where is he?"

E.T. pointed upward. "Beyond the beyond."

"Odd place for a friend."

E.T. stared sadly into the whirling eye. How could he explain that friends are arranged by fate, and dis-tance nothing? "He is very special."

"How?"

E.T. thought a moment, then said, "He introduced me to Gum."

"Who is Gum?"

"Gum is a wizard. Great Gum permitted me to blow bubbles in which dreams are seen." E.T. elon-gated his neck, head rising up. "Gum's world is beautiful, I saw much inside his bubble before it exploded all over my face."

The Contentment Monitor's whirl intensified. *Must do something here,* it said to itself. *Have to cheer this fellow up, get him smiling again. A bubble, eh?*

A large multicolored bubble rose from the Monitor's whirling form. "How do you like *that?*" asked the Monitor proudly.

"Truly wonderful," said E.T., not wanting to hurt the Monitor's feelings.

"So you feel better now?"

"Much better."

"Excellent," said the Monitor, and whirled away. *Not a very tough case at all. I wonder what the Contentment Council could have meant when they said the Doctor of Botany was deeply troubled?*

At sunset, E.T. and his Flopglopple walked home, through the reddish light. Agricultural machines floated overhead like great black beetles, buzzing back toward their maintenance depots, where Micro Techs would attend them.

The Flopglopple looked toward the forest cautiously. "The Urumolki—the Fearful Potencies of Night—will soon emerge," he said, as they approached the vast wood.

"They are no worse than what I faced on Earth," said E.T. "There I was chased by giant shadows bearing rings of shining teeth."

Nonetheless, both E.T. and the Flopglopple changed stride as they entered the forest. Upon a great planet, where enormous power is focused, dark spirits will gather from deep space, and they are the Fearful Potencies. No technology can subdue them, nor is wisdom sufficient when crossing their path.

E.T. listened as the last agricultural machine glided above the treetops, its sound slowly fading. The forest path was dark; and on both sides he could feel the Fearful Potencies, like a faint pressure. The Flopglopple jumped around E.T.'s neck, and hung there like a bunch of woolly gray socks.

"Come now," said E.T., "you're an evolved being."

"I keep forgetting," said the Flopglopple.

"No one will harm us tonight."

A gigantic shadow leapt in front of them, and E.T. screamed, his neck going up.

Watch this one, said the shadow, and took another immense leap, along the path.

"Silly Jumpum!" shouted E.T., lowering his neck in embarrassment. He should have known better, but his own planet was not yet his familiar. He calmed himself, and listened with his inner ear. The Fearful Potencies had withdrawn. Through a crack in the treetops, he saw the Near Moon shining on a craggy mountain range, where the malevolent spirits held their dark rites, conjuring their own vision of the universe, subtle and strange, and real.

"On a planet such as this," said the Flopglopple, "where love truly rules, darkness nonetheless has its way, if only in remote regions, but there most powerfully. There—" He pointed at the mountaintop. "—we will have an encounter."

"No, we won't," said E.T., "for I don't like long climbs."

But the Flopglopple nodded thoughtfully to himself, as if seeing it all quite clearly in his otherwise disorganized mind. Then, all fear forgotten, he hurried on ahead.

E.T. followed through the forest, until the lights of their village appeared, the ring of agricultural gourds glowing. He and the Flopglopple looked down for a long while into the peaceful ring. The Jumpum came up behind them in a silent glide and watched with them. And from the horizon came the lights of the great capital of Lucidulum. "There," said E.T., "the Most High Beings dwell."

You should be there then, said the Jumpum politely.

"By invitation only," said E.T., and knew he certainly wouldn't get one now.

"A brilliant aura," said the Flopglopple, "shining into the atmosphere. That is the power of their intellect."

The waving lights, richly radiant, crisscrossed the sky, the primal powers of the capital expressing themselves. "I might have gone there," said E.T. "I might have tended the splendid gardens of light. But not now. I have up-screwed too badly."

Jumping time! said the Jumpum, and jumped back away into the forest. E.T. and the Flopglopple walked on into the village. The crystals surrounding the village glowed softly, filled with power—a ring-pass-not for the Fearful Potencies.

The Flopglopple raced at top speed past the sign saying *Flopglopples Slow Down,* and disappeared around the back of E.T.'s gourd.

E.T. entered, the door swinging inward on thick fibrous hinges. Three of the chambers were dark, but the fourth, the chamber of contemplation, was softly lit.

There the Parent sat, deep in mental work, engaged in synthesis of sublime thought, by which it would ultimately become a member of Lucidulum's Council. In the center of the chamber, upon a table-tree, sat a round transparent plant; it was called Solis Talla, Shrine of the Cosmos. Within it danced a tongue of flame. How the flame had gotten there, what fuel it burned, E.T. did not know. Botanicus had given it to the Parent as a concentration aid, and the Parent had used it for as long as E.T. could remember, and the flame would dance for no one else, not even for E.T.

But staring at the Solis Talla, E.T. suddenly realized the transparent ball was very much like Earth's great magic Gum. Gum the Wizard! Obviously then, Earthlings knew of such things as the Shrine of the Cosmos, though saying little. *Have some Gum,* was all Elliott had said at the moment of expanding mystery; then the Wizard Gum of the Bubble had appeared, briefly, and departed with a small explosion of His power.

E.T. sat down beside the Parent and gazed into the glowing fire ball. "Gum."

"What?"

E.T. pointed at the glowing ball. "The Wizard of Gum. I met him on Earth."

"The Shrine of the Cosmos is called Gum on Earth?"

"Bubble Gum," said E.T., remembering All.

A faint glow came from the Parent's body as it turned toward E.T. "I have been on the mental wave of the Council of Lucidulum. They say your suspension will be brief, if you can forget Earth. I do not think you have done so."

E.T. looked into the glowing ball, and saw a boy's face. "El-li-ott."

"El Li Ott is of the past. Unreachable. Obscure. A vision in the Bubble of Gum. Lay him aside."

E.T. folded his long fingers in his lap. Easier to forget the whole world than the friend who saved your life. "Owch," he said softly, and swung his feet back and forth under his chair.

* * *

Down the long neck of the gourd he walked, carrying a string of Lumens, the little glowing grubs dangling in the air before him and lighting the way. His room was in the neck of the gourd, at the very end, and was quite small. It held a single bed—actually a shelf engineered from the wall of the gourd and covered with a moss whose fragrance induced slumber and deep dreams. He put his Lumens in a box and closed the lid, and the room was dark, except for faint streaks of red and green glowing in the velvety moss beneath him.

He closed his eyes and immediately a beam shot from his forehead and out through the roof. The little replicant beam streaked through space, into the spiraling arms of the galaxies, through the ominous shadows of the nebula, past the million mighty suns, and down to Earth, into an all-night pizza parlor. The replicant fumbled around, wondering what it was doing in the anchovies, then corrected its trajectory and streaked off down the block toward Elliott's house.

Elliott, asleep, felt his own dream suddenly expanding, into an ever-widening sphere, inside of which he stood, gazing at curving walls. He peered through the thin sticky membrane and saw that he was floating above the bright lights of a city. Then suddenly the bubble rose higher, the city grew smaller, and a gravelly voice croaked, *"Have some Gum."*

"E.T.!"

The dream bubble popped, and Elliott sat up in bed in the lonely darkness.

"E.T.," he said softly, but there was no one there.

He climbed out of bed and walked to the window. He gazed out into the night sky for a long while, hoping for the dream to return, but it had vanished back into its own land, which was dark and impenetrable.

He lowered his eyes, to the lights of the neighborhood. The streetlamps glittered in a long winding chain down the hillside and into the valley. He pulled his jeans on over his pajamas and climbed out the window.

He dropped lightly into the backyard and wheeled his bicycle quietly out of the drive; and then he was pedaling down the street, in the stillness of the late hour. The chain of lights led him on, across those invisible boundaries that divide neighborhoods, and he found himself in other territory, marked for him by a very special feeling—for it was where Julie lived.

He rode along, until he came to her house, and he rode on past it, hoping she'd be at her window as he had been, and looking out. She'd see him and realize what a mysterious person and lone rider he was, pedaling along in the middle of the night on a secret mission. It was so secret he himself didn't know what it was.

"Julie," he whispered as he rode past.

He rode to the end of the block and rode back. The

gentle night air held something so achingly beautiful he could hardly stand it. Entranced, he gazed off toward her house again and his bike rammed into a tree. He spilled off, into a nearby pile of garbage cans, tipping them over with a tremendous clatter. Lights went on in Julie's house and he scurried away, taking a long dive into the bushes.

The front door opened and he saw Julie's father, in his bathrobe. Then he heard Julie behind him, asking, "What is it, Daddy?"

"It must have been a raccoon," said her father.

Yes, thought the lone rider crouching in the bushes, it's just me, the raccoon.

Please don't let them find my bike, please...

The front door closed, and he waited until all the lights were out again, and then he snuck his bike away.

"What am I doing out here anyway?" he asked himself, as he pedaled back through the neighborhood.

The gentle spring night, with its warm perfumes, suggested several very good reasons, but he just couldn't deal with it.

"I was out for a ride, that's all. I like riding at night, when the traffic is light. And I'm making an energy survey of how many people leave their porch lights burning."

He continued pedaling along, through the soft warm shadows.

At dawn, E.T. stepped from the cottage and saw a spaceship rising on the horizon, launched from Lucidulum. Its special signal, like no other, reached his heart.

"Yours?" asked the Flopglopple.

"I feel the thoughts of my shipmates," said E.T., looking at the craft as it rose like a miniature sun.

"Bound for a far world," said the Flopglopple. "While we—"

"The manure pile." E.T. gazed at the rainbow of his ship, his spirit soaring with it into the unknown. He forced himself to move, toward the fields.

"Morning exercises!" said the Flopglopple, stretching. "Isometrics, hard as I can." He stretched his arms out and they simply elongated, no tension possible in them, so flexible were his skin and all his joints. "Ah, that feels much better." He snapped them back to normal length.

"You are an odd creature."

"My brain is loosely hinged," answered the Flopglopple. "Sometimes it slips into my toes."

They hitched a ride on a low-flying Planter, the machine slowly floating by, its belly a mass of furrowing and drilling tools. The machine skirted the forest, just above the leaves.

"The Conjugal Trees are just waking," said the Flopglopple and pointed to the intertwined branches below. "Emanations of deep love fill the morning air."

The floating Planter came in over the misty morning fields.

"Here's our assignment," said E.T., and he and the Flopglopple dropped off among the rows of Alata Nimos, the Wool Spinners. "Like the Conjugal Trees," said E.T., "they seek embrace with each other, through thin pollen-bearing threads. Crossed with Rotum Luxo, an energetic plant whose nature is to twist ever round and round in search of bees, the Wool Spinners now weave their threads in coils that grow ever bigger."

"The birds want the wool for their nests," said the Flopglopple, nodding upward. "And the mice make little carpets," he added, nodding downward at little scurrying shadows.

"We must help the threads the wind has broken," said E.T., walking down the row. As he bent over a little pair of plants at the end of the row, a tall rustling specter sprang at him, filling the air with a hideous shriek. E.T. fell backward, as agi Jabi, guarding the field, waved its crackling arms. Its yellow crystal eye-bud was open, sparkling brightly.

And it thought to itself: *A magnificent screech, that one. They probably heard me all the way to Lucidulum.*

"Must you?" asked E.T., lifting himself slowly out of the dirt.

I must, said agi Jabi.

It folded itself back into silence, and E.T. crept cautiously past. The head of Botanicus appeared over the rows, and he greeted E.T., then studied him carefully for a moment, his eyes penetrating deeply. "Your mantle of wisdom is dark."

"Re-entry is never easy," said E.T.

"Come here," said Botanicus, and drew him into a rock garden between the rows, where a cluster of small plants grew, their buds closed by sheaths that seemed to curl into tiny fists, clutching tight the enclosure of the fruit.

"The Cryptoania," said Botanicus, "whose blossom waits a thousand years. Then a secret unfolds, concerning the destiny of our planet. The Cryptoania alone, of all living things within our world, can feel such designs. Its secret is patience."

Botanicus walked on. E.T. remained before the tightly curled bud. Many years before, at the completion of his doctorate, he'd drunk the tea of the Cryptoania and his innermost brain chamber had opened, itself a cryptic bud of Cryptoania. He'd thought then that he would always be content, for he'd seen his place in the universal scheme and known that he alone was himself, that no other could ever speak to the stars as he spoke, and that this was true for all.

The universe lived and died, in all its immensity, within each single heart, even the heart of a Flop-glopple.

The creature looked at him now, lovingly stupid, without whose love and stupidity the universe would cave in on itself.

E.T. gazed on at the Cryptoania, and one tiny finger of the tightly balled fist seemed to move.

A sudden flash ran through him, wild, difficult to decipher, indeed almost unthinkable. To contemplate it made him tremble all over. His destiny, so the Cryptoania had whispered, was to defy the Most High Lords of Lucidulum, and the will of the planet itself.

The Trompayd's golden horn flower was still covered with morning dew, and its petals had not yet unfolded. "Faster," said E.T. to his Flopglopple. "We must finish before the Trompayd plants awake."

The Flopglopple increased its efforts, scooping up soil, patting it in place. E.T. looked down. The Flopglopple had hilled one of its long rootlike toes and was smiling at it, very pleased. E.T. explained to him that planting one's toes was not the purpose of their work—and during this explanation, the sun pierced the mist, and what E.T. had been trying to escape took place. The shiny Trompayd petals opened to the sun and the entire row of Trompayds let out a deafening blast, brassy and bright, to greet the sunrise.

"Owch!" cried E.T., holding his ears, as the Trompayd blossoms quivered, cheek-like petals blown out toward the sun as they trompayded.

In the distance, a faint drumming sounded, from the hill of the Timpanum plants. This signal, of Trompayd and Timpanum, quickened all the gardens of the morning, powers waking, soil humming, and E.T. felt his secret fate quickening too.

"Why must I be the planetary rebel?" he asked the Flopglopple.

"Perhaps you are like me," said the Flopglopple. "You enjoy stirring things up."

"But I don't. I like smoothing things over. I like my feet up on a sofa, eating peanuts."

"Nonetheless, you are not like the other botanists," said the Flopglopple. "I have always known this about you."

E.T. worked along, most upset. If this fate, the edge of which he'd spied, were ever to unfold, he would not just be farmed out, he'd be cast out, forever, from the planet itself.

"A strange thought attends you," said Botanicus, appearing beside him in the row.

E.T. quickly wrapped a mental sheath around himself, black and thick, folds impenetrable to all—except Botanicus, for whom it was transparent, like leaves held to the sun, through which he saw the mad configuration in E.T.'s brain. "There have been voyagers like you in the past, dear Doctor, who fell victim to the narcosis of the stars."

"Yes, Botanicus."

"There is one, closer to you than you think, who himself was so intoxicated, in a vanished eon."

E.T. looked in the limpid eyes of his teacher, in

which all experience seemed to reside. "You?"

Botanicus blinked, his eyes reflecting an ancient pain, so old now as to be but a shadow, yet there, still there, through eternity. "I loved, as do you, a creature from another world."

"And now you are free?"

They walked together out of the row, and Botanicus pointed to a bed of aged moss. "Dry for hundreds of years. But a drop of water will revive it, and it will become green again, and bear fruit."

* * *

From the row where he toiled, E.T.'s thoughts went out hour after hour, their destination Earth. They hit brick walls, garbage cans, delivery trucks. Finally, the Flopglopple secretly focused his fingers into a scope and sent E.T.'s thought-wave through it. The wave connected with Elliott, in an alley behind the school, where a ring of boys had gathered. Elliott was in the center of the ring, fists up, and an angry look in his eyes.

"G'wan, Elliott, knock his block off."

The circle closed, and Elliott's opponent came after him, fists flying. Elliott felt the blows land, but he didn't feel E.T.'s thought-wave land, though it made a direct hit in the center of his forehead. He was too busy hitting his opponent.

"...punch his lights out..."

"Gettim, Elliott."

E.T., light-years away, closed his eyes and wondered why Elliott couldn't hear, when the beam had struck so directly on center.

The Flopglopple looked at E.T., and listened in on the communication. "Growing up."

"What?" E.T., startled, looked at the Flopglopple.

"Getting older," said the Flopglopple, and resumed his digging.

"Growing up, growing up, growing up." E.T. paced the row, terribly upset, for when people on Earth grew up they lost their wisdom. On the Green Planet, here in the Seventh Nebula of Galactus, as you grew up you got wiser. On Earth, for some reason, when young creatures matured, they lost their secret rulership and became slaves, fools, and blew each other to pieces. He'd seen it on the 6:30 news.

"My friend is in danger. He is about to become the most terrible thing of all. He is about to become Man."

The path seemed to undulate like some great glistening reptile in the dark. But the scales of the serpent were clusters of Lumens, bred by Botanicus to feed along the edges of the path, so that it would always be lit for travelers from the fields.

Overhead, the planting and harvesting machines floated lazily back toward their depots, and E.T. and the Flopglopple were following the path in that direction, to the maintenance depot.

It was a large lighted area run exclusively by Micro Techs. The buildings, therefore, were not simple nobbley gourds, but sleek domes of gleaming metal. Nor were they lit by the homey glow of Lumens; powerful beams of light shone everywhere.

At the depot's heart was the Micro Tech Club, where the frenzied little beings went to unwind; its dome was decorated with bands of colored laser light, and music could be heard coming from its windows.

"I'm trying to restrain myself," said the Flopglopple, his tripod of feet scratching frantically in the ground. "But I *can't!*" And he raced toward the Club, went through the doorway in a blinding rush, and disappeared within.

E.T. approached more slowly, across the hard surface of the depot, a plane perfectly flat and lifeless, the way Micro Techs liked things, so as to avoid the unpredictable, such as flowers growing in one's way, but it was not E.T.'s way; his fingers trailed dully along over the inhospitable surface. Ordinarily he wouldn't go to the depot at all, but tonight he had a reason, and it was one that made him fearful. Slung over his shoulder was a kitbag, with a small bulging object inside it.

"Well," he said to himself as he came to the doorway. "I've *got to party.*" With this Earth phrase to brace him, he squared his shoulders and entered.

The inside was as sleek as the outside, everything metallic and shining; tables were crowded around a small dance floor, where the Flopglopple was already gyrating with other Igigi Gyrums, their lithe slender bodies snapping madly, their tripodial feet moving in a blur. Music came from a gleaming little bandstand, and there a Fluteroot was swaying, playing its heart out; it was accompanied by a Trompayd, the Trompayd's brassy golden cheek petals swelling out as it blew. A pair of Timpanums, their taut drumhead blossoms beating like rhythmic hearts, kept an intricate beat. The plants were all potted, in large containers provided by the management. Flashing colored lights ringed them, and these plants did not play the gentle music of the groves; theirs was the wild, exotic music of the capitals, of Lucidulum and Crystellum.

Seated at the various tables and almost oblivious to the music, were the Micro Techs, arguing as always:

". . . unrelated to the recognizable properties of the system . . ."

"No, no, it's a simple defection of A and D!"

"Stop, you're choking the definition!"

"I'll choke *you!*"

Their transparent little heads glowed bright red as they shouted, screamed, and banged on the tables, their enormous round eyes popping.

"I'm sorry but you've left out position, energy, and atomic weight."

"A priori formulation! Fraud!"

"I cling to the original metric."

"Yes, well, you might as well cling to a bedpost."

For all their technical brilliance, their diminutive stature made them argumentative, and as a rule, quite rude. E.T. made his way through their tables, at which they sat on high stools, flailing their arms. And when he passed, one of them leaned toward him, squeaking, "Adverse ratio? Dissimilar magnitudes? Capsule eject, eh? Kicked off the ship?"

E.T. ignored the jibe, for he had bigger things on his mind, strange and frightening things—the matter of his planetary destiny, already shaping his footsteps.

He skirted the dance floor, where a handful of young Jumpums were bouncing up and down to the beat; they came to the Club in their early years, before they grew too big to get through the door. And beyond them, E.T.'s Flopglopple was flopping madly to the beat, his long loose arms tied in bizarre knots with his partner.

E.T. made his way to the bandstand. The Fluteroot tooted above him, swaying in its pot, and the Trompayd bent back, blowing a high sweet passage. Seated on the edge of the flashing pot was a Micro Tech, playing the fifty string a'lud, each string as thin as a hair; his own hair-like fingers, countless in number, picked over the strings in a blur, producing the most intricate sound imaginable, the sound of his own compressed and complex soul.

This was Micron, the only Micro Tech E.T. was friendly with, from a voyage made long ago, to a planet whose musical enchantments had affected Micron and changed him, and made him an outsider. His fifty string a'lud was from that planet, and remained the source of his enchantment.

He opened his eyes now, saw E.T., and joined him on the floor. They took a table together, off in a corner. Its smooth transparent surface was lit from within by a changing pattern of light, suggesting approaches to infinity.

"I hear you've had bad luck," said Micron.

"It's probably going to get worse."

"Why?"

E.T. lifted his long neck, craning it high and looking around to see if he might be overheard. Then he lowered it and leaned in toward Micron. "I'm going to borrow a starcruiser."

"An interesting thing to do," said Micron, and he too looked around, for ears that might have come too close. But they were alone in the crowd.

"Will you help me borrow it?" asked E.T., his

voice now no more than a hoarse whisper as he leaned still closer, the lines of electric infinity reflecting on his ancient face.

Micron drummed his many fingers on the table, the whole of them looking like handfuls of nervous spiders. "And where would you go in a borrowed starcruiser?"

"To Earth, the Blue Planet."

"Never heard of it." Micron gazed slowly around the room, his round eyes taking on a faraway look as they reached the bandstand and rested upon his a'lud. "There's only one planet I wish to see, and you know what it is."

"Shadoma Rubi?"

"Shadoma Rubi, the Planet of Song. Yes, for that I would risk a great deal." Micron reached for his a'lud and strummed it thoughtfully. "For it is where I live, in my heart." His a'lud sounded, with a soft and melancholy air, as if calling across an impossible distance. E.T. listened, and knew the feeling.

"You will help me?"

Micron ceased playing, set his a'lud on the table, and became the brisk, officious Micro Tech he was supposed to be. "My friend, the ships of Lucidulum are the most advanced of vehicles. To merely start one takes a lifetime of study."

"I was mistaken then," said E.T., and made as if to rise from the table, knowing that no Micro Tech can admit to not understanding anything technical. "I assumed you had the knowledge—"

"I know what I know," said Micron. "But the ships of Lucidulum know much too. You don't just walk up to one and say, let us go." He leaned forward now, his own voice falling. "The ship itself would sense our approach, long before we got near. The ships of Lucidulum are—alive."

The two friends fell silent then, and the music from the bandstand floated around them, vegetal and strange, rising from the unknowable depths of the Trompayd's tap root to eternity. The Fluteroot's mellow reed sound joined it, and the Timpanums rumbled with them, all of it sewing the air with the ineffable, and E.T. felt it twining itself around him.

Micron looked back at him. "Yes, there are mathematical facts for which there is no explanation. These fools—" He nodded toward the other Micro Techs in the room. "—think they can argue their way to solution, but the Mind Holders alone, the great mathematicians of the Fleet—they alone know its secret."

"Botanicus will know."

"A vegetable wizard," scoffed Micron. "We're discussing High Radiation Cruisers."

E.T. stared down into the electron patterns flashing in the table. The mission, he knew, was beyond him. What could a plant doctor like himself hope to know of synchrophotonics? Of velocity and the stress of the wormhole vortex? He might as well try to get to Earth on a bicycle.

"Nonetheless," he said to Micron, "if I make the attempt, are you with me?"

"It's an impossible undertaking," said Micron. "I must say no."

"I have with me," said E.T., opening his kitbag, "a new beverage. I learned its formula on Earth. It is called beer. Would you care to join me?"

"Always interested in new concoctions, Doctor."

*　　*　　*

E.T. walked home in the light of the Near Moon and the Far, their glow casting twin shadows everywhere. "We are two-mooned too," said the Flopglopple. "Both wisdom and ignorance pull at our soul."

E.T. looked at the creature, but the Flopglopple had returned to silence as he flopped along, examining the night.

Between them was Micron, whom E.T. had given several bottles of his home-brewed beer, which he knew could change one's point of view dramatically—a situation he wanted to bring about with Micron. It had worked, perhaps too well.

"Wonnerful, wonnerful," stammered Micron. "Beer, you say? Most amazhing drink . . . hiccup . . ." The little creature waved his filamental fingers in the moonlight, thin threads entwining, combining, releasing, like some dream-plant of shadows.

He staggered forward, attempting to strum his a'-lud, which was strapped around his neck. ". . . play anything . . . fixsh anything . . . *fly* anything . . . hiccup . . ." He fell down in a little heap, unconscious.

E.T. and the Flopglopple picked him up, E.T. saying, "I am filled with guilt for what I've done, for a headache of some magnitude will attend Micron's awakening. Is it right to do such things to a friend?"

"He doesn't seem unhappy," said the Flopglopple, looking at the stupefied grin on Micron's face.

They carried him to the outer edge of the depot, where the Micro Tech barracks was situated. It was a genuine Micro Tech creation—a construction of maddening detail, built with a thousand clean and perfect corners. Disorder of any kind troubled Micro Techs deeply and the building was spotless. Even in the darkness, a Micro Tech stood admiring it, drawing comfort from all the sharp, angular lines leading to more of the same.

"If they could," said E.T. to the Flopglopple, "they would arrange the leaves on trees, putting them all in a neat pile at the top."

Micron woke, thrashing, as they approached the barracks. "...one more sip...of...of..." He passed out again, and E.T. and the Flopglopple snuck him inside.

The corridor was sleek and shining. Micron's room was small, bare, and frighteningly neat, as are all Micro Tech quarters. A bed unfolded automatically from the wall as they entered, and the covers rolled down with a faint mechanical whisper; the pillow fluffed itself out, until every wrinkle vanished.

"Set him down gently," said E.T.

Micron opened his eyes, winked, and said, "I'm with you, Doctor...hiccup...count me...count me—"

"—out," said E.T., as Micron's head rolled to the side and a tiny snore escaped his lips.

The door flew open and a Micro guard bristled in. Micron woke and waved. "Goo' evening, offisher. We're having a...a little feshtival of the arts." He reached for his a'lud and fell, out of his micro bed, onto the floor.

"What is going on here?" snapped the officer of the guard. "What is wrong with this technician?"

"...feshtival...fesh..." Micron began to crawl around beneath his bed.

"He has just come from—the Jaws Man," said E.T. "He had a tooth repaired and his gums and tongue are numb."

Micron rolled on his back, fingers waving gaily, like the legs of a drunken centipede. "...modelo tar bu (he sang)...modelo tar bee..."

"He appears to have gone mad," said the guard, frowning darkly. He looked at E.T. "And who, may I ask, has dental work done in the middle of the night?"

"I do," yammered Micron, grabbing the edge of the bed. "I love night dentis'shry." His fingers went limp and he slid back down on the floor, dragging his pillow with him.

The guard stared with wide blinking eyes, then snapped his gaze around the immaculate room. "This compartment is a mess. Unbelievable sloppiness. And *he's* a mess." The officer of the guard looked at E.T., and his frown suddenly deepened. "Aren't you the demoted Botanist First Class? Put off ship?" He drew himself to his full height near E.T.'s knees and snapped, "Creating more havoc here, is that it? Spreading your influence? I order you to leave at once."

"...give 'im a beer..." croaked Micron, clutching his pillow.

"Out!" shouted the guard.

E.T. and the Flopglopple backed out of the room, and then scurried down the hall.

"I think," panted E.T., "a pattern is developing— of my being—constantly in the soup."

"Purely—mechanical—reasoning," answered the Flopglopple, as they raced into the barracks yard. "You are an infinity of causal factors, only some of which—lead to the soup."

But E.T., as if possessed by just those factors, stopped and tipped over a trash barrel, which he knew would drive the compulsive Micro Techs into a frenzy. "Hollow Bean!" he shouted, and raced with his Flopglopple, out of the depot.

A joyous surge of telepathy shot from his brow and sped toward Earth. Owing to E.T.'s erratic style, his telepathic replicant went through Earth's atmosphere fluttering and darting like a knuckleball, and descended toward a used car lot where Honest Monty the Used Car King was selling an elderly woman an automobile that had been owned by a dragster named Cameron "Cam" Shaft, now deceased. Its frame had been bent into a right angle by a bus, but had been cleverly repaired by Honest Monty's spot welder.

"Yes, ma'am, this little gem was owned by a woman like yourself, who never drove it farther than the supermarket on sunny days."

"Well, I *do* like these fancy flames painted on the hood," said the gray-haired woman, gazing through her trifocals.

"Yes, they're quite decorative," said Honest Monty, "and—"

And E.T.'s replicant landed, on Honest Monty's shoulder. Honest Monty blinked, and gazed at his elderly customer. Suddenly it was as if his own dear mother stood before him, for E.T.'s replicant was crawling down his shirt front, over Honest Monty's heart. "Ah, Mother, I mean ma'am, actually I have a better car for you over here—"

"Does it have flames painted on it?" asked the little old lady.

"I'll have some painted on for you, dear. This car is much more suitable."

The little replicant dropped to the ground, looked around quickly. It only had so much thrust and no more, and must find Elliott before its energy was drained. It shot away in a streak of faint rainbow light, and reached Elliott's house with a dying charge. But it found its way in through a window, to Mary's room, where Mary was just putting on her imitation pearls, and taking a last look at herself in the mirror. Her date was due to arrive any minute. He was a computer engineer, very attractive and intelligent, although his conversation tended toward the discussion of disc-drives, terminals—and modems, which she'd made the mistake of thinking was a new rock and roll group and had told him how much she'd liked their latest record.

"However," she said to herself as she left her room. "I'll be better company tonight." She'd had Elliott instruct her in matters of software, and felt suitably prepared.

The replicant followed Mary out of the room, its energy failing fast. It slid down the banister beside her, confused about its mission, feeling only a great but diffused love for the occupants of this familiar house. It was supposed to merge with one of them, merge and communicate . . .

"O.K., gang," announced Mary, as she stepped into the downstairs hall, "may I have your attention, please?" She felt she should tell them who her date was, explain some of his background, reassure them that their mother was not going out with just anyone. "Alex will be here in a few minutes and—"

"Yeah, Mom," said Michael, not hearing, head buried in *Sports Illustrated*. "Have a good time."

"—and I've told him all about you and about your interest in modems."

". . . um-hummmm . . ." said Michael, concentrating on the biography of a seven foot center with elbows like andirons. "... enjoy yourself."

"Michael, you're not listening to me."

"Sure I am, Mom. Modems." He turned the page.

I'm searching for a *new father* for you, said Mary to herself. Isn't that important?

She saw that it wasn't. Her children were adjusted to things as they now were, to a one-sided household with herself at the center, trying to keep it from flying apart. Her dates were traumatic only for her, not them.

"Hey, Mom," said Elliott from behind her, "did you remember everything I told you?"

"Yes, Elliott, I've achieved computer literacy."

"CPU?"

"Central processing unit."

"Bus?"

"No, Alex has a car."

"Mom!"

"Oh, sorry. The bus carries signals to and from the microprocessor."

"Alright," said Elliott, "now don't blow it."

"Thank you, dear."

I love this child, she thought, looking at Elliott, and I want him to be happy. And he wants me to be happy. And why do I feel like crying when I see him rooting for me, that my date should be successful and I don't perform like a dumb terminal with Alex? She leaned down and kissed Elliott on the forehead. "You're a good teacher, Elliott."

E.T.'s little replicant jumped from the banister, toward Elliott, trying to deliver the message but Elliott moved and the replicant landed in the umbrella stand, message nearly forgotten in any case, all of it fading now, like a dream from another world.

"Company coming!" cried Gertie from her post at the window. "He has curly hair and a little black beard and a box of candy and he's taller than Mom and he—"

"Thank you, Gertie dear, that's sufficient." Mary walked toward the door. "I won't be late, children."

"Take your time, Mom," said Michael. "Don't worry about us."

"You may have a *few* of your friends in. *Not* entire neighborhoods."

"Got it, Mom."

The way he says that, reflected Mary, I know hordes of teenagers will be in here, until five minutes before I return. But what can I do?

She opened the door. E.T.'s replicant leapt desperately from the umbrella stand, missed Mary, and landed on Alex's forehead. Alex stared at Mary, blinked slowly. "I just had the most astounding realization about linear address decoding."

"I'm sure you did, Alex," said Mary, and took him by the arm, turning him around on the doorstep. She had the feeling it was going to be a scintillating evening at the data bank.

From the horizon, at noon, came a sudden eruption of light—first red, then yellow, then blue, above the distant capital of Lucidulum. The sky filled with the colors, which spread like a canopy, shell-shaped, as if some genius of the sea had gestured. And from the heart of Lucidulum came the faint sound of its populace intoning a chant, half murmur, half song.

"A Mind Holder has been crowned," said Botanicus, "with the Wreath of Wisdom, Final Rank."

E.T. gazed at the radiant canopy, which was the energy-mind of this new Lord of Lucidulum, now a cosmic power, a principle, primal and complete.

Botanicus nodded, as his students gathered around.

"In that direction, toward such a moment, do you all progress. One day, thousands of years hence, you shall yourselves be crowned, without exception." He turned toward E.T., and lifted an eyebrow. "Well, perhaps with one exception."

* * *

Micron piloted a tiny, low-flying service capsule, which the Micro staff used for repair runs around the farming region. E.T. and the Flopglopple rode scrunched up in back with the tools. Micron had an ice-pack on his head. "Each time I turn my neck, just slightly, a stabbing pain—here." He pointed to his temple.

"On Earth," said E.T., "it is called a hang-over."

"Yes, that is how I woke, hanging over the edge of the bed." Micron shifted his ice-pack. "I don't think I will drink more beer if it can be avoided."

"It is not strictly necessary," said E.T. "On Earth we sometimes drink another drink. Gertie made it for me. It is called Kool-Ache."

"I do not think I wish more ache than I now have, Kool or otherwise," said Micron, again adjusting his ice-pack.

The little pilot banked the service capsule and began descent; a moment later the vehicle fired its landing jets and the craft settled down in a small clearing in the hill region. The transparent hatch of the capsule opened, and the three crawled out, E.T. and the Flopglopple dropping down on the ground behind Micron.

"This is the region of the ancient mines," said E.T. "Why have you brought us here?"

Micron said nothing, only smiled and led the way

into the hills. Stone piles, from early excavations, lay everywhere. It was a barren place, dead as an airless moon. "From another time," said the Flopglopple, "in the beginning."

E.T. looked around the desolate landscape, and saw a number of Tickli Moot-Moot plants, tall and slender and possessing the peculiar characteristic of making a laughter-like sound; on most occasions they could be heard chuckling softly to themselves, and always in the most remote and inhospitable places— as if they were there for the purpose of cheering a cheerless surrounding. Tickli Moot-Moot, or, Continuously Tickled Plant as it was known in the handbook of wild flowers: and here it stood, typically, in a stark landscape as gloomy as any one could find.

"But they aren't chuckling," said the Flopglopple, listening closely, his ear extending from his head on a long elastic trumpet-like protuberance. "No, not even a giggle."

E.T. walked around the clump of silent Moot-Moots.

Thirst, we are . . . dying of . . . thirst, said the plants, but E.T. knew it already, from a dozen signs.

It has not rained . . . in seven double moons, sighed the plants. And they gave a choking, tortured chuckle, though it was no laughing matter, but laughter was the only sound they had, produced when their flowers opened to attract a nectar bird whose call was also like a laugh. But the nectar bird had not been here for a long time, for the nectar was dried to dust, as E.T. could plainly see as he peered into the fragile, wilted blossoms.

"Come on," said Micron. "What are we standing around for? These plants are dead."

"One moment," said E.T., and turned to the Flop-glopple. "Find a rain crystal, quickly."

"Rain crystal, rain crystal—" The Flopglopple sped off, tripodial feet a blur. Only when running at top speed did his keen intuition begin to work; when the scenery was a blur he saw things inside it, and so it was now, as it rushed past him in a flickering dance, within which he saw the secrets of the terrain.

"... buried caverns ... veins of metal ... silver ... gold ... nothing useful there ..." He sped even faster, streaking in a great circle around the landscape. Suddenly, he put on the brakes.

"Rain crystal." He screeched to a stop and dove at a slide of loose rock. He yanked the rocks aside, and revealed the glowing crystal within, its face dark, darkened by the stormy potency within it. He pried it from the rock and rushed back with it to E.T. and the Moot-Moots.

"Rain crystal!" He handed it to E.T.

"You are a splendid Flopglopple," said E.T., and set the crystal in among the Moot-Moots.

Why have you disturbed me? asked the crystal.

"Dying Moot-Moots," said E.T.

Hadn't noticed, said the crystal. *Busy, you know.*

"Well," said E.T., "we'd appreciate a—"

Spot of rain. Yes, quite, said the crystal, and concentrated.

A cloud appeared over the hilltop, and then another, coming like fluffy animals called by their master.

Right down here, said the crystal. *Parched Moot-Moots.*

The clouds sailed in, and dropped low, so that suddenly E.T., the Flopglopple, and Micron were standing in mist, which swirled all about them.

A soft chuckling was heard. It was answered by a rumbling from the clouds, and then the rains began. E.T. and his crew danced out from under the shower, which confined itself solely to the Moot-Moots.

"Interesting demonstration," said Micron. He looked at E.T. "They teach you a few things at the gardens, I suppose. *We* have electronic cloud-makers at Micro Tech Headquarters. Make you sheets of rain any time you like. But this wasn't a bad show, if a trifle old-fashioned."

E.T. nodded his head at the Moot-Moots, satisfied they'd now survive, and he resumed his march, following behind Micron. "I'm receiving a signal," he said, "a dark one."

"From there," said Micron, and pointed to a shadow in the hillside. As they approached, E.T. saw it was the opening to one of the abandoned mines, millennia old.

But just beyond the shadow of the opening was a heavy metallic seal, blocking the shaft from entry.

"Locked," said the Flopglopple.

Micron studied it for a moment, then ran his spidery fingers over the face of the plate. "One of the old electron locks, simple enough if you know how." His fingers worked, emitting a steady stream of squeaks and beeps of the electron code. The plate grew suddenly incandescent, and itself began to squeak and beep, and a moment later it became transparent, and then vanished altogether.

A dank, damp smell rose from the passageway.

"I feel a powerful presence," said E.T.

"I too," said the Flopglopple. "This shaft is not going to be merely an empty channel carved in rock."

And the Flopglopple, who by nature always propels himself headlong at full speed into new opportunity, stepped cautiously into the shaftway.

Micron drew a laser torch from his little tool case, and it cast a bright beam into the darkness ahead.

"There's the old descent tube," he said, pointing to a cylindrical shape in the rock ahead of them. Dust and webs covered it, dulling a finish that had once been bright. But, thought E.T., that was so long ago; he would have to open deeply buried layers of his memory to recall what had once transpired here, and who had engineered it.

Micron ran his fingers over the face of the descent tube and a control panel popped open, cobwebs and dust flying up from it. The little technician examined the line of gauges. "Pressure is still good. Everything functional, nice bit of work, made to last. Well, come aboard." A door swung open in the tube, more dusty webs breaking apart. E.T. and the Flopglopple stepped inside.

Photoactinic light filled the tube as Micron closed the door, the light emanating from an ancient tentacled Lumen, whose radial arms undulated with a brilliant internal glow. The tube was its eternal prison, wherein it shone for itself, and for no one.

Micron was testing the interior controls. "System's a little sticky, but I think it's safe enough." He pressed a button, and E.T. felt an almost imperceptible movement, but a glance at the gauge showed they were descending at a very high speed.

The Flopglopple looked around with great interest and saw a distortion of himself on the curving inner wall, head greatly elongated. "Pressure P on corresponding volume V?" He pointed at his head, thinking it had actually shaped itself into a cone, which he thought very handsome.

"A reflection," said E.T.

"Reflection," mused the Flopglopple, but kept feeling his dome hopefully, as the descent continued.

And then, smoothly, it stopped. The door opened and they stepped out. Owing to the great depth, the gravitational field had altered, and the Flopglopple took an enormous leap, twiddling his tripodial toes in the air.

They stood in a rock gallery, whose roof arched high overhead; at the far end of the gallery, light and shadow moved.

"My frontal lobes murmur with expectancy," said E.T. "The inner layers of memory have spoken, and I know who dwells here."

"Yes," said the Flopglopple, whose own memory had dived deep. "We are in the realm of the asteroid miners."

Micron nodded. "The outlawed ones."

"Who visits?" A rough voice echoed in the gallery, and a figure moved from the shadows. It had a large head, which, even in the poor light of the cavern, could be seen to be strangely formed, and while its body was not much larger than E.T.'s, it was clearly from another branch of the planetary family.

Micron stepped forward. "We come as friends," he said, voice echoing through the gallery.

"Friends?" The figure took a step forward. "We have no friends. Approach cautiously, intruders."

E.T., Micron, and the Flopglopple moved slowly down the gallery, only the Flopglopple remaining gay and unperturbed, his footsteps still enjoying the lighter gravity, as he continued leaping up and down, toes twiddling. E.T. felt a current, magnetically potent, sweeping the gallery.

The asteroid miner's head was hard and faceted, like a gemstone. "But where are your arms?" asked the Flopglopple, perhaps impolitely, and staring at the creature's odd-shaped body—a long, mummy-like cylinder of blue and purple, faceted as was his head.

He is an ancient amalgam, thought E.T. His kind is wrapped in mystery. E.T. noticed then, that the creature's head reflected light, as do the precious gems. Its eyes, like its head, were glowing, a crystalline lattice radiating at the center, the lattice moving, pulsing regularly.

"A living relic," said the Flopglopple, dancing around the creature, who apparently was able to tolerate the Flopglopple's innocence. "Primeval design," continued the Flopglopple, scrutinizing the being's head and body closely. "Metallic laden. Creates heat and life through electromagnetic field, needing little food or oxygen to sustain it. You feed on—?"

"Metals," growled the ancient creature.

"Ah," said the Flopglopple, nodding its head and looking around the gallery. "And so your natural home is close to those veins, yes, yes, I see."

"Do you?" asked the creature sardonically, and E.T. saw that its crystal eyes reflected lost dreams, of the former eon, when metallic beings had ruled, and gathered the metals of the moons and the diamonds of the comets, and ravaged the planetary system with war.

Sudden apprehension filled E.T. More trouble would result from conspiring with such a being. I'm liable to find myself in a jam, a pickle, and the dog home.

"We've come to seek your help," said Micron.

The creature's faceted head flashed, the facets each bearing a moment of light, before it moved back into the shadows. "This way."

The subterranean being led them into a second gallery, a vaulted room with furniture of stone, comfortable enough for a creature able to ingest metals, but E.T. thought a cushion of moss would help considerably.

The room was lit by radial Lumens, tentacles glowing as they crept along the walls and ceiling. And the feeling of the place, despite its cold rock walls, was one of deep security, for in fact, thought E.T., we are deep, and not likely to be disturbed. No one at least, will overhear our plan. The Contentment Monitor does not descend here.

"What can I do for you upper world beings? What use have you for an old miner?" The creature leaned back in its stone chair, and again the facets in its head flickered with an internal light.

"We need a flight crew," said Micron, "to get us through the warp of time. And you've piloted big ships in the past."

The old miner studied his guests more closely now, and an orange-yellow luster filled the crystal lattice of his eyes.

E.T. felt an emanation of material desire coming from the being, and he leaned forward to clarify the mission; and his tongue naturally chose words he'd learned on Earth, their destination. "We're not after—" He paused, to get it correctly. "—big bucks."

"You're after what you're after," said the old miner. Now it was his turn to lean forward. "I am called Occulta. I used to fly the great starcruisers of the former eon. And I'm at your service." He smiled, and a drop of mercurial substance dripped from his lips.

* * *

Occulta took them deeper, down a corridor of hewn pillars. Streaks of gold ran through the rock, entwining the pillars like garlands.

"Another being ahead," said the Flopglopple, scurrying forward, toward a third chamber, in which he disappeared. E.T. and Micron followed, with Occulta, into the chamber, where they found the Flopglopple gazing at its occupant.

The creature's head was disconcertingly like E.T.'s, as if showing clearly where once the two lines of evolution had been one. But the differences between them were also profound. E.T. studied the armless shape. Where had he seen such a thing before?

The Flopglopple provided the answer. "A large bulb of garlic," said the Flopglopple, examining the rotund sheaths of the creature, each of them like a separate clove. But instead of the fragile skin of that plant, the creature's skin was armor plate, and no knife could ever peel it, that was certain. It meant to endure, and had provided for itself accordingly.

The eyes, though superficially resembling E.T.'s, had a quite different characteristic—they were metallic mirrors. E.T. peered into them, trying to find their expression, but saw only himself in miniature, approaching. The creature spoke:

"Look yet more closely, visitor. You'll find all you know and love in my eyes, for you will always find yourself." And he laughed cynically, a dark laugh, dark as his body, whose inner sheen was silvery, the vessels of his life-flow bearing streams of the precious ore. E.T.'s frontal lobes filled with archaic patterns, of a cold metallic reign, where once this creature had been a prince. That reign was over now, and its prince in exile beneath the world.

"I am Sinistro," said the mirror-eyed old sovereign. "What business have you here?"

"They wish to recruit us," interjected Occulta. "To pilot them through the warp of time. We know it well, eh, Sinistro?"

They laughed together then, and suddenly their bodies expanded, blossoming outward in the most astonishing way. The metallic folds lifted, like petals, raised from within by long thin arms, hidden until now.

They are like flowers, thought E.T. But they were not gentle buds in blossom, but the opening of fierce warriors. Their lifted sheaths revealed a pulsing interior core, charged with magnetic power. Inner ribs, supporting the lifted sheaths, were shining. The long tentacle-like arms gestured in archaic sign language, and E.T. felt the creatures' magnetic centers merging in a single powerful field. He leaned toward the Flopglopple and whispered, "Such beings are not to be taken lightly."

"But their cold metallic nerve is what is needed now," said the Flopglopple.

However, added E.T. to himself, I must be cautious, for many a jam pickle could result.

Sinistro smiled, and the surface of his mirror eyes glistened. "Can it be? That those of the upper world have need of their banished brothers?" His mirror eyes flashed, and E.T. saw himself trapped in their gaze.

"B. good." He raised his finger gently toward the old asteroid miner.

"Good? Why, of course, of course." Sinistro raised his own finger—a sleek black digit shot through with silver streaks, which streamed profusely for a moment, and E.T. knew it as the power of the subterraneans, those at the core, who listened to the planet's innermost rumblings; their love of its grandeur and violent beauty had shaped their reign—a time of terrible upheavals and drastic fissures in the social fabric. How did he dare bring them to the surface?

He turned away, confused and uncertain, deep in the forbidden cavern. Why was he always the one to whom these notions occurred—to peek in windows, to make beer and borrow a starcruiser? Why?

Sinistro draped an arm around his shoulder. "A visitor, the first one to come and see us in centuries. I'm deeply touched. I'm overjoyed." His mirror eyes shone with cold indifference. "I'd thought we'd been forgotten by all."

Sinistro's bare, rock-like chest suddenly glowed with spiraling whorls of silver.

His heart-light, thought E.T., and his own heart answered, glowing ruby red. Sinistro stared at it, as at a gem he desired for his collection.

* * *

Occulta and Sinistro led the way to a fourth chamber, where the last of the subterraneans dwelled. He too was seated on a stone couch, his figure perfectly still. But his eyes, like quartz crystals, pulsated, and E.T. saw that the gaze was awake, and felt it examining him minutely.

I am Electrum, said a telepathic voice.

The crystal eyes sparkled and Electrum rose. He stepped toward his visitors, and the Flopglopple rushed to examine him. "A toadstool without a stem," said the Flopglopple, studying Electrum's squat shape. "Yes, with an umbos on top." The Flopglopple was pointing, rudely perhaps, at Electrum's bullet-shaped head, growing out of his mushroom-like body. But this was not a delicate forest fungus creature. His flesh was armor, his head a battering ram capable of crushing and shattering anything in his way. His mouth slowly opened, as if with great effort, as if ages spent in the solitary darkness of these caverns had cost him the use of speech. But then a voice, cavernous as the vault which surrounded him, slowly sounded.

"Welcome—to the depths."

Only in the eyes did he show any kinship to E.T. and the rest of the planet, but it was a remote kinship at best. This being had carved a different road for itself in the bygone times, gone under the world, had made his home in planetary interiors.

He looked at Sinistro and Occulta, and all three of the beings expanded together, their metallic folds lifting like flowers, flowers of the caverns, alien to light and thus generating their own; their bodies glowed now, as their tentacular arms gestured in the lost signing of long ago, by them alone remembered. Occulta, Sinistro, and Electrum conversed in silence, and then, once more, their metallic sheaths were lowered and their wild forces were concealed.

Electrum turned to E.T. "So—you have your crew."

Two moons lit the landscape, and the twin orbs caused the forest to be crisscrossed with many shadows—among which some very special ones were moving stealthily.

"There it is," said a soft voice.

The starcruiser sat on its launch pad in the moonlit valley, in the hills beyond Lucidulum. Artificial light blended with the glow of the double moons. The pad and its surrounding base were lit by flood towers, and by runway markers, the entire bowl of the valley divided into bright patterns of many colors, each color defining a specific area. Micro Techs swarmed over the cruiser, attending to its needs.

"Ants," snarled Sinistro, "crawling over a shiny apple."

"That's the Matter Converter they're working on," said Micron.

"Photon rocket." Sinistro lay beside him in their hiding post in the hills. "Design hasn't changed much since the old days." His black finger pointed, a swirl of silver fluid illuminating the tip. He turned to Occulta, whose own body had begun to glow with internal energy, purplish-blue.

"Yes," said Occulta, "we know it well. Or well enough." He turned to Micron. "We must observe it for a while as it comes and goes. In the meantime, Doctor—" He turned the other way, toward E.T. "—you can work your own plan. Eh?"

"O.K.," said E.T. in Earth jargon, the words coming naturally to him now, for he'd had time to contemplate the language and knew all its delicate shades. "Sex and rock and roll," he added, to further clarify his position.

Electrum moved his toadstool-like body along the edge of their hiding place, so he could see the aft portion of the ship. "Our old designs have never been bettered. That ship can travel forever, refueling itself from the matter of the stars."

The vast arena, with the ship at its center, seemed to gaze back at them with its myriad eyes. The crew members came and went, preparing for a night lift-off. Their shape was like E.T.'s, but almost transparent and much more fluid, for theirs was the most evolved form—pure mind in a thin membrane, which altered its shape according to need—two arms, then three, or four, then none, the shape becoming a simple, elegant sack of intellect in repose. Now, approaching the ship, they were bipedal, legs moving easily, their arms gesturing with great delicacy, fingers long and expressive, through which the moonlight passed.

"Mind Holders," said Occulta. "An airy bunch."

"How can they stand it," said Electrum, "to have no metal in their veins, no force fields, no charge? Why—" He looked at E.T. "—even this vegetable doctor has a live current in his spongy frame."

E.T. gazed at the Mind Holders, whose learned ways he admired above all things. They were far beyond him. They knew the innermost layers of the supreme sciences, were creatures of enormous patience and power, and he was going to borrow their starcruiser. Much, much rock and rolling would be needed to outsmart them.

The Mind Holders entered the ship, their forms altering into sheer technological states as they disappeared into the corridors. The Micro Techs closed the hatch, their million fluttering fingers sensing every micrometer of the seal. Other of their colleagues were already on board, at their posts, micro-tuning the liftoff navigation systems, and bringing the mighty craft to its first stage of power.

"Yes," said Sinistro, "worth creeping out of the ground for."

The launch pad was clearing now, the last of the Micro Techs leaving the hull of the ship, and withdrawing to their command pods—gleaming balls spaced around the ship, from which they would activate and monitor its final stages.

One by one the command pods lit up, until a pulsing ring of light surrounded the starcruiser. Within it, in control of the manual system, the Mind Holders were concentrating, and a familiar glow suddenly filled the windows of the flight deck, a light like the one

E.T. held in his fingertip and heart, but brighter by far, a blaze of the purest subtle energy.

And then, at another window, in a section of the ship most familiar to E.T.—the Botanical Wing—a face like his own appeared.

"Owch," said E.T. softly, as he saw his fellow botanist in the position he himself once held, off to gather flowers of space, for the universal garden. How he missed it, the calyx of love, the mercy of the world, plants giving life its bubble of air on planets near and far.

"Ah, she's beautiful," said Electrum, staring at the cruiser as its first stage fired and it lifted upward.

The invisible gases suddenly thickened in a rainbow of color, the high temperature exhaust wearing all the splendor of the cosmos, and then the ship was lost in it, accelerating into the upper darkness.

E.T.'s thoughts went with it, in a telepathic signal soaring through the heavens. It navigated the labyrinths of stars, and came down, nearly on target. Elliott was at the park pool, getting set to show off with a fancy dive. Julie was seated at the edge of the pool, legs splashing back and forth in the water. Her bathing cap was shaped like layers of flower petals, and E.T.'s little replicant landed in them, thinking she was a large white rose. A funny feeling went through her, as the replicant touched her, a feeling of something faraway and strange. And it had to do with—Elliott.

She turned toward him. He'd walked to the edge of the diving board and was extending his arms. He raised them, sprang off the board, and sailed into the air with a tremendous bound, peaked and turned over, arms flailing; he came down flat on his back with a loud *splat*, and sank like a stone.

Julie pushed off the edge of the pool and swam over to him as he surfaced, glassy-eyed.

"Are you alright?" she asked.

Water was running out of his nose, ears, and mouth. "Sure, sure," he gasped. "I was just—experimenting. Testing the board."

"Testing it?"

He looked at her, at the little wisps of wet brown curls coming from under her petaled cap. The little replicant leapt from the petals toward Elliott, but its diving form was worse than Elliott's and it landed near the filter drain, which started sucking it in. *Help*, cried the replicant, and the lifeguard turned his head.

Did I hear somebody yell for help?

He scanned the pool but there were just two kids in the water, Elliott and Julie; the others were playing around the edge. The lifeguard returned to contemplating his suntanned navel, and Elliott swam toward the ladder, doing his famous Australian dog paddle. Julie glided beside him, with lithe graceful strokes. "Are you going to test the board again?" she asked, teasingly, as he held on to the ladder, still gasping for breath.

"Yeah," he said, for he *did* have one more fancy dive in his repertoire, where he grabbed his knees and went in like a bowling ball. He wished he were a swimmer, a great swimmer. *Oh, if only I had a teacher.*

El-li-ott, cried the little replicant, fighting against the pull of the drain, and thrashing in the water.

Elliott turned his head, but there was no one there, only a few rainbow reflections glittering on the water's tossing surface.

"Let's swim together," said Julie. "We'll do the sidestroke."

"Sure, fine," said Elliott. That was the stroke in which he sank sideways and got chlorine up just one nostril, an old favorite. But he swam beside her, looking into her eyes, and for a moment he thought maybe her toe had just touched his. A thousand thrills ran through him, and he heard other voices at the pool as if through a dream. He gazed at her and wished he had the guts to play a big love scene, but it was better to remain hard-to-get, so he rolled over and switched to his Olympic backstroke, the one where he sank *gradually*, like a submarine.

She followed him, sleek and coordinated, a natural athlete, in the pool, the gym, the field, was drawing closer to him again, and that meant he must draw farther away, to keep her guessing.

Nearby, the little replicant fought with its own best stroke against the suction of the drain, but it was caught in the whirling water and filtered out of the pool. It angled through the pipes, the pump, the hoses, and began to expire before circulation was complete. Only a fragment of its energy remained, a faint fading shape incapable of affecting anything, and when the filter spat it back out, it was just a bubble which popped and disappeared.

"Guess I'll go now," said Elliott, climbing up the ladder of the pool.

"I'll come with you," said Julie.

"Suit yourself," he said, and wondered why he couldn't say what he really felt. But it was impossible. No way. Greg and Tyler would have too much fun at his expense if he ever got hung up on a girl.

But whose life was it anyway?

"I'll just be a minute," said Julie, as she went toward the girls' dressing room.

He watched her go, and then knew what his next move had to be. He grabbed his bike, and still in his bathing suit, he pedaled away, clothes jammed in the basket, water flying off him. He smiled inside at the thought of what she'd say when she found him gone.

Smooth, Elliott, *very* smooth.

E.T. entered the transparent dome. Row after row of exceedingly odd plantlife was displayed, and the air was heavy with scent. "This," said E.T. to the Flopglopple, "is where Botanicus raises his rarest blossoms."

"They reach upward," said the Flopglopple, "supplicating the sun."

E.T. looked at him and wondered, as ever, about the true nature of his supposedly silly companion.

The Flopglopple looked back. "Coated with cutin," he said, knowledgeably and seriously, as he pointed to a leaf. "Water and gas proof," he added. But then he took some beard moss and hung it from his chin, and made a stupid mustache with the rest of it.

E.T. entered the rows of the Yaa Iram, the Fire Plants, who sat in flame proof pots, solar flowers hanging from their stems, incandescent gases licking at the air. Of blossoms, these were the most desirable, and for their protection, they were simply too hot to handle.

"Yaa!" cried the Flopglopple, hopping around, beard moss burning, fingers singed by the Yaa Iram.

"This way," said E.T., entering the next row, of Rak-heshma, the Veil Plants. Their gauzy petals undulated in the air, permitting only a fleeting glimpse of the inner face of the plant, whose buds, like eyes, winked open and closed. "Let me see," said the Flopglopple, but the plant hid its face most cleverly.

"Here is the Cloud Bearer," said E.T., admiring a plant with its own prominent pedestal at the end of the row. "Unlike the chuckling Moot-Moots, it can never die of thirst."

The Cloud Bearer's stems and leaves were surrounded by tiny puffs of cloud, from which tiny insects came and went like birds in the firmament; a tiny rumble of thunder came from the cloud and it began to rain on the soil below.

"It waters itself!" cried the Flopglopple. "I must do that! I must have my own cloud, and rain on myself whenever I want a drink, as I'm frequently thirsty from rushing around so much."

"These are the hybrids," said E.T., "created by Botanicus for his own amusement, and for gifts to the courts of Crystellum and Lucidulum."

As he spoke, E.T. suddenly filled with longing, to see the courts again, where the most exotic creations of all were exhibited.

"In the court of Crystellum," he said to the Flopglopple, "there is a plant called Nahf Natika, the Crystal Night Sky Plant, in whose spherical, transparent bud tiny constellations burn, and wandering planets pass, hour after hour, until the sphere opens in a single burst, sending the gleaming little seeds in eccentric orbits, to fall, and grow more Crystal Night Sky Plants."

The Flopglopple was trying to scoop handfuls of cloud around his head. "Stay there...b. good..." But the clouds kept floating back to the Cloud Bearer.

E.T. went deeper into the dome, and the Azra Uttus, the Winged Blossom Plants, began to flutter at his approach; petals flapping, their many flowers floated into the air, and they landed on E.T.'s head like a crown of butterflies. Not wanting to hurt their feelings, he let them stay on his head as he wandered through the crowded aisles, which were a confusing riot of color.

The Wing Blossoms fluttered, and tickled his ears. He hardly noticed, for he was searching for something—

—which used to be here. Where has it gone to?

He scratched his head and the Wing Blossoms fluttered onto his fingertips, and then flew away, all of them, in a long line that shot in and out of the aisles and trays and came to rest like a pointer over the plant he was looking for.

Of all the plants in the hothouse, it was one of the oddest. Every part of it, instead of lifting its leaves and flowers to the light, drooped limply downward as if wilted—an impossibility in any garden of Botanicus, where all the plants were perfect specimens.

E.T. smiled. This was it.

The droopy-looking plant had two especially long branches that hung into the dirt like arms, and the rest of its shape gave the impression of someone very tired, asleep against a post; the uppermost blossom, in fact, emitted a tiny snoring sound, petals moistly fluttering. From this blossom, E.T. took a tiny pinch of pollen, a disturbance which caused the plant to shift, like a person turning over in bed, but the snoring continued.

"And what brings you here, Doctor?" The voice of Botanicus came softly behind E.T., who popped into the air with a little jolt of surprise. He turned and slipped the bit of pollen to his Flopglopple, who took it, and slid back under a bench, out of the reach of Botanicus.

"I'm visiting the plants," said E.T., backing away from Botanicus.

"They seem happy to see you," said Botanicus, nodding at the Wing Blossoms who had once more fluttered back onto E.T.'s head, where they fanned their wings slowly up and down.

"I've got to—buzz off," said E.T.

"Are you a bee? Strange words flower on your tongue," observed Botanicus, as E.T. continued to back away.

"No stranger than the blossoms which surround me," said E.T., feeling his way toward the door.

"Your mind, like my plants, is now a hybrid? Of the Blue and Green planets?"

"My mind is—*all zonked.*"

Botanicus stepped closer, but E.T. was already out of the door, and proceeding down the path with his Flopglopple, who still held the handful of pollen in his palm.

"What is this?" he asked E.T.

"It's from the Shemoda Nuncoor, the Sleeping Princess Plant."

"And what does its pollen do?" The Flopglopple brought his fingertip to his smiling mouth. His tongue tasted the golden dust, and a second later he was asleep on his feet, toes pointed out. A loud snore broke from his lips and he swayed back and forth, and finally crumpled to the ground.

E.T. shook him by the shoulder. "Rise and sign. Up and atom."

The Flopglopple lay where he was, snoring deeply. E.T. sighed, slipped his arm under the Flopglopple and slung him over his shoulders. Staggering under the burden, he marched off, the Flopglopple still asleep, drooping down his back.

*   *   *

Out of the constellation of Nebo, an uncharted star appeared, growing larger. "Here it comes!" cried Sinistro, rising from his place in the forest.

The falling star became a brilliant sphere, descending through darkness, vapor trailing. Its lateral jets fired and the ship was trimmed, its descent path straight to the landing pad in the canyon. It seemed to leap between the moons, grew enormous, and glided down over the pad, where a swarm of Micro Techs awaited it.

In the hills, at the rim of the canyon, Sinistro paced excitedly, his metallic folds opening and closing with nervous bursts of energy. Electrum was beside him, and Occulta, the three dark princes of the underworld lit by the momentary glow of the descending spacecraft. "She's a ship of rose and gold," said Sinistro, his gaze, long buried in the labyrinths, now widening and remembering. "She's what a chieftain needs!"

"True, true," said Electrum, his quartz eyes pulsing, as the ship's magnetic field touched them in its descent, its great energy stores firing, landing jets coming on as it lowered gently down.

"It shall be ours," said Occulta, and turned toward E.T. "Thanks to our little doctor of greenery, eh?"

E.T. stared fearfully at the three princes of the underworld. Their electric intensity had increased here upon the surface, where the storm winds blew. They were wild now, pacing, their metallic folds billowing out, their laughter edged with a desire so ancient he'd forgotten how fierce it was. These were former masters, accustomed to power, and denied it too long.

Sinistro put his arm around E.T. "Did you get your special plant? The one you spoke of?"

"The Sleeping Princess!" sang out the Flopglopple, who'd finally awakened. "Shemoda Nuncoor, for a good night's rest." He flopped around dreamily, twiddling his noodle-limp thumbs. "I had a dream of running so fast I met myself coming the other way."

E.T. looked at Sinistro, Occulta, and Electrum. "I have what is needed." He pointed to the launch pad below. "I can control activity there."

"Excellent," said Sinistro. "And now come with us."

E.T. and the Flopglopple followed the dark lords to a crevice concealed in the backward slope of the canyon. In the space of a single afternoon, the old mining experts had widened and deepened it, so that it had become a staircase of stone, leading to a chamber in the canyon, which they'd carved into their headquarters. Observation niches, cut into the canyon's face, looked directly down on the launch pad.

"We're safe in here," said Sinistro.

"Don't you find the ambience of rock much friendlier?" Occulta gestured to the cold, stark stone interior. "And from here—" He stepped to the observation niche. "—we shall monitor the great ship of Lucidulum, until we have unraveled its secrets."

"Some of the new technology has left us behind," said Sinistro. "But we shall learn quickly. Look, look at Electrum's eyes!"

They were pulsing as always, but now they'd filled with myriad points of light, connected in a pattern. Micron stood before him, and looked into the eyes. "Navigation circuitry. Is it—?"

"The starcruiser's," said Sinistro, pointing through the niche to the launch pad below. "Electrum has tapped it telepathically."

"Electrum knows how to listen," added Occulta. "His body resonates with things when he so desires. And his eyes reflect what he hears."

"I can see the ship's entire first stage sequence," said Micron.

Electrum sat perfectly still, only his eyes animated, electrical messages flowing within them, as he listened to the starcruiser's secrets. His body was as the stones around him, motionless but not lacking in perception; he flowed, out through the stones into the air, and then inward to the heart of the ship. His voice came in a whisper:

"Delicate surveillance down there. This I feel too. The ship knows it has been penetrated."

"But it hasn't known the likes of us within its recent program," said Sinistro, smiling.

He sat upon the stone couch, beside Electrum. For a moment his body remained animate; but then it suddenly stilled, deeply so, the mineral elements of his nature, those that were cold and patient, taking over. He became as still as Electrum, as he directed his gaze upon the second hole cut in the rock wall. E.T. and Micron saw a flutter of energy flow from his head, and then in a flash it sped out through the rock wall. His eyes, pale mirrors, grew suddenly bright. "Ah," whispered the old pirate of the stars, "what sublime power they use down there."

His mirror eyes flashed with reflections from the ship's master computer, its reaction chambers, its energy extractors.

Micron looked into Sinistro's mirrors. "He's linked with the ship's drive—all settings can be extrapolated from this." Micron began to figure, and his transparent little body filled with whirring mathematical formulas.

Occulta's metallic cloak opened, traces of electromagnetism trailing from it. "Orbital speed, spiraling sunward." He smiled, closing his cloak about him and seating himself on the couch beside his concentrated colleagues; a moment more and his posture became like theirs, like three ancient figures carved in bas-relief, in a lost cave on a time-forgotten planet.

"Handy fellows," said Micron, as he continued to make calculations from their eyes.

But E.T.'s eyes had grown deeply troubled. The alchemy of the dark princes was directed at the ship, which to him had always been like a flower of the sky. Now that flower was about to be plucked, violated.

He drew the Flopglopple aside. "I've been trapped by these old sorcerers."

"Permit me," said the Flopglopple, "but wasn't it *we* who went calling on them?"

E.T. nodded grudgingly. Events were his responsibility. "I want to end the matter. Let this plan dissolve back into the night."

The Flopglopple gazed closely at him, eyes squinting at E.T.'s forehead. He touched it. "A transmission signal is forming in your brain. Through axons and synapses. I see it speeding off, and time opens."

E.T. felt it also then, a telepathic current moving independently from his head. It pierced the dimensions, passed its twin sister, Light, and found the magnetic field of Earth.

The din was tremendous, of anger, greed, and folly. Within this din was Elliott, trapped in the net of Earth's madness. "His identity is already blurring," said E.T.

"Yes," said the Flopglopple, tuning in to the transmission. "He is no longer constant with himself. He is becoming just another dull pattern of conformity."

"El-li-ott," whispered E.T., desperate to save his friend. He looked at the Flopglopple. "I must disregard the consequences."

"I always do," said the Flopglopple.

Their conversation was interrupted by Occulta's arm snaking out from between his folds. His head flashed suddenly; then the light vanished from his head and emerged from his extended fingertip. A beam of laser intensity fired at the rock wall, the searing beam cutting a perfect rectangle from the stone. The chunk of stone fell to the chamber floor, and starlight appeared through the smoldering hole. A comet plume appeared in the sky, sailing past.

"A comet like that—we catch it, implant a thousand megaton explosive, and mine the interior. For jewels, my friends, the most precious food!"

He fell silent again, and Micron continued monitoring the information-filled eyes of the three immobile princes of the underworld. But he was stopped suddenly by a sharp clacking sound that came from the dark lords of metal. The sound was repeated, and Micron scratched his head. "Iron reeds closed by a magnet, wasn't it?"

The magnetic clack came again. Their heads glowed, Sinistro, Electrum, and Occulta flashing simultaneously and light began to weave and merge directly above them.

"The star of Nebo," said the Flopglopple softly.

A transparent globe formed from the projected light. Rolling from their heads, it grew and filled the rock chamber. Its shimmering surface began to crackle with electric force, and snake-like bands of energy wrapped around it, as if holding it in shape.

"High energy enclosure," said Micron, nodding. "Old Magic, isn't it?" he asked E.T. "From the Former World?"

"Yes," said E.T. gravely. "It is an earlier power."

The bubble shimmered, and then, within it, more substantial objects began to appear—a command seat, an instrument panel, a second seat and matching panel, with switches covering the inner surface of the bubble.

"A replica!" cried Micron. "Perfect, look at the detail!"

"The flight deck of the ship," said E.T., staring into the energy enclosure, where the flight deck was appearing.

The Flopglopple flopped forward and extended his finger toward the bubble. A spark leapt from it and caught him on the nose. "Yaa!" The shock ran through him to his toenails, on which he now hopped up and down in distress. "Dod-gamma, that hurt. Owch, owch, owch..."

"Look," said Micron, pointing but not touching. Within the energy enclosure, three figures were taking shape, perfect replicas of Sinistro, Occulta, and Electrum, except pale, and transparent. Outside the bubble, where the three old pirates actually sat, the light in their bodies was dim, all their energy streaming out into the bubble, where simulacra of them were slipping into the control seats. Ghostly fingers worked the switches and set the launch circuits working.

"They're activating a mental lift-off," said Micron.

The bubble began to glow with brilliant force, like the ship of starlight itself. E.T. felt his spirit lifting with them, into night, space, the track of far worlds.

Then, quickly as it had come the bubble exploded, its enclosed images vanishing too, and the three lords of darkness slumped forward on their stone couch, exhausted by the energy it had cost them to manifest the bubble. But one glittering mirror eye of Sinistro opened, and a metallic smile crossed his lips. "We held her soul. We know her secret."

"So, Doctor," said Sinistro to E.T., "what's on this planet Earth to which you so desperately want to go? What kind of treasure can we expect?"

E.T. thought for a moment, in the stone lair, the outlaw band seated around him. "One day you might have your own—closet."

"I would like that," said Sinistro, pretending he understood. "Indeed, I cannot wait to have my own closet."

"And a football helmet."

"Yes, naturally, I must have one of those."

Electrum leaned forward, eyes flashing. "What about me?"

"You might have your own TV set," said E.T.

"Truly wonderful," said the dark lord, gold and silver streams of excitement showing within his metallic shell.

Occulta leaned toward E.T. "And I? What shall I have?"

"Your own bicycle," said E.T.

Occulta nodded, not wishing to appear ignorant before his colleagues. "That's as it should be. Good, very good."

E.T. looked at the three old miners, at their hungry mouths and lustful eyes; he'd stirred the banished emotion of greed, and formed a scheme for its destructive waves.

I fear, he said to himself, I am once more involved in a terrible up-screw.

* * *

E.T. and his Flopglopple crept slowly down the hillside. The Near Moon was only a crescent and the Far Moon had not risen at all, and the forest around them was dark. Ahead, through the trees, the lights of the launch pad gleamed, rectangular multicolored patterns blinking on and off, as the base cycled through its constant program, all of it rayed out around the ship of starlight itself.

"I dreamed we had a spaceship," said the Flopglopple, "but it was a strange one."

"Shhhhhhh," said E.T.

The Flopglopple put a finger to his own lips, and reminded himself to be quiet. "Shhhhhhh."

E.T. shifted his mental wave to the modality of green, photosynthetic layer. A lush and succulent mental wave answered him, and his body turned directly and automatically toward it.

"Faint tendrils brush over my mind," he said to the Flopglopple softly.

"Yes, mine too," giggled the Flopglopple, "very ticklish." Then, remembering he must be more quiet, once again he put a finger to his lips, saying, "Shhhhhh," to himself.

"This way," said E.T.

"The wave grows stronger," said the Flopglopple. "Like a leaf wrapping itself around me."

"It is the food of the Mind Holders," said E.T. "It sends out these mental waves."

"There," said the Flopglopple, "through the trees."

Ahead were several square acres of paddy, where the refined substance grew—a hybrid of Bazmat Lizoona, Brain Plant of the Jungle. "No food is more powerful," said E.T., "nor so refined as that which grows here."

The crescent of the Near Moon was reflected in the water of the paddy, upon the gelatinous slick that was the plant's virile substance.

"Its power rises in a mist," said E.T., pointing to the wisps above the paddy. "It is lured by the moonlight."

"It feels our approach," said the Flopglopple.

"It knows me," said E.T. "I am one of those who bred it."

The mist of the plant had begun to reach toward him, the wispy tendrils caressing the revered doctor, so instrumental in creating the present and most sublime strain.

Taste me, said the plant, for in the tasting the plant felt itself fulfilled, metabolized through the mental centers of the taster.

"Bazmat Lizoona," said E.T., quietly addressing the mental spirit of the paddy, "I've brought a new nutrient for you."

He crept forward, into the shadows surrounding the paddy. The two moons shone their slender crescents on the still waters, and the lights of the launch pad were only a glow in the sky beyond the treetops.

E.T. opened up a pollen pouch. "I have brought you Shemoda Nuncoor, the Sleeping Princess." He emptied the pollen pouch into the arms of Bazmat Lizoona. An ecstatic tremble ran through the gelatinous substance of the paddy.

"A new hybrid has just been made," said E.T. to the Flopglopple.

"And tomorrow the base will dine on it," said the Flopglopple.

"In these refined organisms, all process is heightened and quickened," said E.T., as the trembling of the gelatinous mass continued, spreading from one side of the paddy to the other. A sound like sighing came from the thick viscous substance. E.T. crouched, for the sound was a loud one, and carried a strong signal, of a quivering Brain Plant. Would the caretakers hear and come running?

He heard no approaching footsteps. He nudged the Flopglopple and they crept away quietly, back toward the woods. But the Flopglopple tripped over the root of a Jumpum tree, and shook the tree awake.

Jumping time!

The Jumpum leapt up, woke its friends, and they all shook their leaves and danced.

"A jumping contest," groaned E.T.

They stuck out their roots and turned, waved their branches and came back, toeing, footing, tapping, their boisterous rustling filling the night air.

"Back to the paddy," whispered E.T. frantically to the Flopglopple, and they raced back to the paddy, where they each scooped up a handful of Shemoda Nuncoor. Then, racing back to the Jumpums, they stuffed the sleeping potion down the Jumpums' knotholes.

Sleep-y, said the Jumpums. They stopped, stretched, swayed back and forth dreamily, and then nodded off, branches drooping. And E.T. and the Flopglopple continued their retreat through the woods.

The launch pad was now visible through the trees, with the starcruiser at its center, portholes beaming. E.T. turned to the Flopglopple.

"How do I dare think of putting myself in command of such a thing? I'm no hero of the cosmos."

"You're very good with geraniums," said the Flopglopple.

"I nap on the long voyages. Or play checkers." He lowered his head and continued shuffling along. "What is to become of me?"

"Waves of probability can't be seen," answered the Flopglopple.

They continued along the dark forest path, the starship still faintly visible through the trees. Then a sudden rushing of their senses told them—the ship was about to fly. A low whirring sounded, and a moment later light was streaming through the forest, as the ship began to lift off. E.T. and the Flopglopple craned their necks back as the ship cleared the treetops. Its main thrusters filled the air with rainbow gases and it shot straight up.

"On the path between Lakama and Oto," said the Flopglopple, pointing to the twin luminaries of the first boundary of space. The ship, like a comet, sped between them, and then was gone beyond the reach of the naked eye.

E.T. and the Flopglopple hurried on, their path taking them out of the woods and in sight of the rocky face of the canyon where, like slitted eyes in a giant's face, the niches of the hidden grotto watched all that passed. Behind the niches sat Sinistro, Occulta, and Electrum, and E.T. could feel their concentration, could almost see the beams of their powerful focus as it swept the launch pad, spying out its inner workings.

"Hurry," said E.T., which is not a word you have to say twice to a Flopglopple. The creature whizzed away, up the rocky trail of the canyon wall. E.T. followed, lifting his feet carefully, so as not to trip in an undignified manner on his head. A Doctor of Botany must be well balanced and set a good example. By borrowing a priceless starcruiser. I must be mad . . .

A telepathic beam rose from his brain, and sped out between the twin stars of Lakama and Oto. Passing the first, second, and all successive boundaries, the tiny beam found its way to Earth, off by about 20 degrees, powerful but erratic, like its sender. It landed in the TV section of a department store, where twenty-five TV screens suddenly showed a silvery ghost, with duck feet and a long neck, crowned by an eggplant-shaped head.

"Sumpin' wrong with yer sets, mac," said a shopper, as channels began flipping in a rushing pattern, while the little mental replicant tried to find its way out.

"I assure you, sir," said the department head, "there is nothing wrong with these sets."

"Yeah, sumpin's flyin' around inside 'em, bugs or sumpin'." The customer, who had to purchase a small set for his drinking den, a place of cosmopolitan grace, gave one of the sets a kick.

"Please, sir, these are not used cars."

"Sometimes a kick straightens 'em out." The customer, who made submarine sandwiches for a living, adopted his electrical engineering stance. "Wakes the old tubes up." He took a set in his hands and shook it violently. E.T.'s little beam was bounced out through the back. "Yeah, that's better," said the sandwich engineer.

Set free in the store, the tiny glowing replica of E.T. was wondering where in the name of heaven it was.

"Come on, Gertie, we've got to buy you some galoshes."

A familiar voice sounded in the aisles. The telepathic replicant turned, little neck rising up, toward Mary, as she dragged Gertie along.

"I don't *want* galoshes," said Gertie. "We don't even *call* them galoshes anymore."

"What do you call them?"

"Designer boots."

"Well, *I'm* calling them galoshes," said Mary.

"I hate them."

"You'll learn to love them. All little girls learn to love their galoshes."

"Only if they're yellow. And I'm not little anymore."

"Sir, do you have any yellow galoshes?"

"No, madam."

"See," said Gertie.

"See what?" asked Mary, beginning to grow bewildered as she always did when shopping for her children; another hour and she'd be babbling in the aisles, in the common tongue of mothers. Then I'll yell at Gertie, Gertie will start whining and digging her heels into the carpet, and I'll be one step from the Child Abuse Center.

"Please, Gertie, be cooperative, we're going to buy *green* galoshes."

"Yuck."

"Thank you, sir, galoshes in green will be fine."

"Very good, madam."

Such a refined salesman, reflected Mary. A good influence for my barbaric children. We'll buy the galoshes and I'll ask him to marry me.

She waited as the salesman rooted through the boot boxes. She'd been seeing more of Alex lately, but he'd proven to be slightly on the manic side, electronically calculating the calories of the meals they ate, and "interfacing" the soup and salad. She was no longer sure if she wanted an alphanumeric relationship. Maybe something cozier, based on footwear.

"Here you are, young lady, try that on."

"Yuck."

"That's right, dear, yuck-green galoshes." Mary gazed down at the salesman's bald head. It's warm and homey looking. I can easily imagine it sticking up over the end of the living room couch every evening.

"There, young lady, how does that feel?"

"Awful."

"We'll take them," said Mary. Because I've got to get out of this store. Not because I almost just now took out my lipstick and wrote *I love you* on this man's head. But also because I just saw a little green creature looking at me. From over in the next aisle.

E.T.'s telepathic replicant was indeed looking on, and now it was following Mary and Gertie through the store.

Gertie pulled Mary into the electronic game aisle, and picked up a Speak and Spell. "Mommy, remember mine?" She held the spelling computer up to Mary. "It's still broken."

E.T.'s mental replicant dove into the computer, and flew through the microchips, rearranging their memory with quick skips of its toes. So when Gertie pressed the Speak and Spell, it said, in E.T.'s voice, *"B. good."*

"Huh?" Gertie stared at it. "Mom, it's, it's—"

"—too expensive," said Mary, and put the Speak and Spell back down on the counter.

"Mom!" cried Gertie.

"Don't dig your heels in, Gertie." Mary yanked her along, as Gertie yelled and hung on to the edges of counters.

"Mom, somebody else might get it, it has a *message* on it!"

"That's right, dear, it says come along with your mother before she pulls your arm out of the socket."

"It was E.T.!"

"E.T. is gone, Gertie. Far away."

Just then, Elliott turned the corner in the toy department, with a very odd look on his face. He blinked, dully, toward Mary and Gertie.

"Elliott," said Mary, "what are you doing here? Don't you have a music lesson at this hour?"

Elliott blinked again. "I had the feeling I'd—meet someone here. Someone—"

"Who?" asked Mary.

"He *was* here!" cried Gertie. "Elliott, E.T. was here!"

Mary went quickly into action, taking Elliott by one arm and Gertie by the other. "Come on, children, let's move it. We've got lots more to do today."

She couldn't let them fall back into fantasies about E.T. Their life was on Earth, not out in space. She had to protect them, against what she wasn't quite sure, but it was no good them dreaming about E.T. For E.T. was like their father—not somebody they were likely to see again, ever.

*   *   *

E.T. climbed over the rim of the canyon. The launch pad, empty now, was below, only Micro Techs left, straightening things up. He continued along the rim of the canyon and found his way to the crevice in the rock. He entered it, down the rough-hewn staircase. Here and there Lumens hung, lighting the winding passage deep into the mountainside, and lighting the grotto where Sinistro, Occulta, and Electrum sat on their stone couch.

The transparent bubble of their concentration was once more floating in the center of the grotto, and within it, as before, was a mental image of the command module of the starcruiser. Micron stood beside the bubble with the Flopglopple, the two of them staring into it, where the spectral forms of Sinistro, Electrum, and Occulta floated, hands on the controls.

"They're with the ship, out through Lakama and Oto," said Micron.

The spectral forms of the dark lords moved on the flight deck, from instrument to instrument, piloting their spectral starcruiser. Then, as the navigation screen showed them about to leave the planetary system entirely, their figures began to dissolve inside the bubble, and then the bubble itself dissolved, control panels and command seats dying into darkness.

Sinistro's physical body slumped on its stone couch, exhausted from sustaining the mind bubble so long, and Electrum and Occulta slumped beside him. Electrum's right eye slowly opened, and the pulses within it were faint. He raised himself up on one elbow and addressed E.T. "A point about which I want to be absolutely certain—" The dark lord's other eye opened. "—we'll each have our own bicycle?"

"I promise," said E.T.

"Excellent." Electrum's eyes closed back up, and a faint smile crossed his lips, as he slumped forward again.

E.T. tended to the old miners, then, putting to the lips of each a tumbler of liquid—the herbal extraction called Voogle Oppep #2, made of an excellent array of vivifying flowers, all lively and bursting with vitality—the Rapidly Ascending Oppep itself, able to climb a hundred yards a day in season; and the five strains of Voogle, whose vine, though slower growing, could, once it had wrapped around a slender tree, bend that tree to the ground, after which it would release its own tap root and it and the tree would spring straight, the Voogle flying off the top and sailing to a new growing site, where it would root once more.

The extract of these plants glistened now on Sinistro's lips, and the old miner brightened and straightened, his energy returning in a smooth natural flow, and he started to rise to his feet.

"You are not altogether restored," said E.T. "You

need this rubbed on your brow," and with his glowing fingertip he touched a spot of salve to Sinistro's brow, and then Occulta's, and Electrum's. Their ragged, exhausted mental auras responded with a quiver, and reshaped themselves, edges firming up into the proper density. "Much better," said E.T., examining the three old miners closely. They protested that they were perfectly all right, that they could make giant mental energy enclosures all day and notice no strain, but they were glad of E.T.'s attentions, for no one had tended them in ages; no one had touched their brow, or cared if they wandered alone forever in their caverns, decrepit and dying. No, this little Doctor of Greenery was different, for they could feel his tender concern, and though they were gruff and violent old pirates, they, like all creatures of planets Green and Blue, responded to kindness.

"Decent little bean-reaper, isn't he," said Occulta softly, as E.T. left them to rest, placing a bag of aromatic herbs in the stone chamber, which would complete his ministrations. A scent, unlike anything the dark denizens of the underworld had ever smelled before, filled their chiseled noses. A pleasant ease came over them, and they fell into a gentle and untroubled sleep, in which they dreamed of a faintly glowing spirit who cared for them, and stroked their brows, and whispered tales of ancient glory, in which they themselves were the heroes, and all was well in their reign. They remembered all, all the greatness they'd once known, and lived it again, and spent the night in such fantastic memories as these, which E.T. made for them, with his herbs of love.

The dining hall of the launch base was slowing filling. A starcruiser had returned to the pad, and its pilots, the Mind Holders, were making their way to a table. Slender, ethereal, delicate, they entered in a group, discussing neuronal networks, but the only sound from them was a hissing undertone, their communication on a higher and more subtle frequency.

The other tables were filling with Micro Techs, whose chairs, of course, were higher. Their manners were deplorable, for they argued fine points of technology and physics while banging their spoons. Loud, boisterous, one might almost say uncouth, the Micro

Techs cared only for the designs of supermicropro-cessors, and the components of linear momentum, the hall echoing with every aspect of these subjects and many others besides.

"Pla! B and T9 with electron volume vom sixtus!"

"Ridiculous! You cannot use the start sequence F in that arrangement, which is essential with the mer-ketron othmak."

"Both wrong! You must look to mass point Tlaskret Sluckk, in the E-field."

"You're all a bunch of dull-witted digit drivers!"

They shouted, were overbearing, and bounced up and down in their chairs. Their thousand-thread fin-gers tied themselves in frenzied knots as they em-phasized a point, and their terribly agitated, high velocity conversation made the dining hall into a buzz-ing hive.

When the soup came, they hardly noticed, just spooned it up while they continued arguing—though it was a delicious broth of Bazmat Lizoona. The soup spilled down their chins, and because they dunked their crackers so violently, their fingers needed to be licked continually clean, which they did, in the middle of their bickering.

And then, while brandishing his spoon, one of the Micro Techs started to yawn. His fingers slowly loos-ened, his spoon fell into his lap, and he collapsed face down in his soup.

A series of little splashes followed, all around the hall, as one Tech after another yawned and fell in the soup.

The Mind Holders, accustomed to gross behavior from the Micro Techs, did not notice that all around them heads were going down. They were engaged in higher considerations, concerning the mystery of corporal teleportation, when suddenly one of them, in the midst of a nonverbal transmission to his neighbor at the table, found his elbow going into the salad dressing. *How terribly inelegant of me,* he remarked to himself. *And now I seem to be falling into a plate of Beeperbeans. Observation: The soup was drugged* . . .

A moment later, his colleagues had also slumped into the salad dressing, and two moments later the entire dining hall was asleep, under the dominion of the Sleeping Princess, Shemoda Nuncoor. In their deep sleep, the Mind Holders saw her, a beautiful veiled spirit of the plant world, spreading her cape over the launch base.

* * *

The Flopglopple flopped along beside E.T., and his gaze kept running over E.T.'s form, which was bent, tired, and very, very sad.

The Flopglopple reflected: Something's bothering the boss.

The Flopglopple reflected some more, and put a toe in his ear as an aid to concentration. I should be able to help him. Running through my brain in profuse if disorderly fashion, are all the great equations of the last one thousand years.

I should be able to apply them.

Instead I have a toe in my ear.

Why?

Because I'm a Flopglopple.

Micron walked beside them, down the canyon path, toward the launch pad. "Don't worry about a thing," he said to E.T. "My logic cells are clicking." His little body pulsed with information, his internal schematic on display. "Yes, all you need is a Tech like me, well schooled, with total absorption, faultless recall, and a handsome, audacious nature."

"Noisy little package, isn't he," said Sinistro, following on the path with Occulta and Electrum. Their forms dominated the path, their metallic cloaks opening and closing as they strode along toward power once more.

"I'll have not one, but *two* bicycles," said Electrum, "and I shall have them set in a necklace so that I can wear them all the time." The old pirate of the stars laughed heartily, as he'd not done for centuries. Treasure, yes, there'd be much of it—bicycles, paper routes, and Gum.

"And I—" thundered Occulta, "—I shall be a Burger King." He pointed at E.T. "Did not the little Doctor of Greenery describe Burger as the greatest of all things in the universe? Yes, I shall be a Burger King."

The three metallic lords strode fiercely forward, down the canyon path, toward the base. The lights of the base were becoming visible now, through the last ranks of the forest.

"Ah me," sighed E.T. to himself, as he looked down at the launch base. Within it, not a soul stirred, for everyone's face had fallen in his soup, and snores filled the air.

I must be deranged, thought E.T., to have done a thing like this.

His mind was confused, divided, remorseful. But each time he thought of Elliott, growing up a galaxy away with no one to counsel him, he knew he must proceed with his reckless plan. "El-li-ott," he groaned softly.

"Who's this El Li Ott he's always talking about?" asked Sinistro.

"I believe he's a ruler of the fabulous planet Earth," said Electrum. "Thus, he would be one of the Burger Kings."

The dark lords nodded together over this obvious fact, for it would be pointless to cross the universe for anyone less than a potentate of Burger. "He will be rich, of course," said Sinistro. "The Earth word for wealth is moo-la. And we shall have it, my friends, much, much moo-la and—a pogo stick." Sinistro smiled at the ignorance of the others, for he alone had been told about the device. "All the great rulers have a pogo stick. It is kept by their throne for times of emergency. Elliott, the King of Burger, has one in his closet. As you know, we shall each have our own closet."

"Truly, this is a mission worthy of our talents," said Electrum.

"The little doctor has told it all," said Occulta. "Earth's treasures are uncountable. The Monopoly Board, for example, which is worth millions, especially the portion called Boardvark. I must tell you, in advance, Boardvark is mine."

Sinistro cast a sharp glance at his companion but said nothing. However, thought Sinistro, when the time comes, we shall see who rules Boardvark, from a pogo stick. Wearing the helmet of Foot, and decorated in bicycles.

Conversation ceased, then, as the edge of the forest was reached. The launch pad was before them, the great starcruiser at its center. In all the attending domes and barracks, lights burned but no one moved anywhere. A heavy silence, punctuated only by the occasional snore, filled the air. Sinistro patted E.T. on the back. "You've done it, Doctor," he said softly.

I've done it, thought E.T.

The Flopglopple edged up to him. "You've broken about a hundred planetary laws in one jump."

"I can't be trusted to water a dandelion now," said E.T. "I'm a criminal." He sagged within, as the full realization of what he'd done came over him. "This is the first act of infamy on the planet in thousands of years."

"Oh well," said the Flopglopple, "I'm usually in trouble."

"No," said E.T., "you are an Innocent."

He gazed at the trees, the sky, the familiar moons, and thought—this cannot be my home anymore. "Once we take that ship—" His gaze traveled to the launch pad. "—we shall be wanderers forever more, severed from home through eternity."

"I don't care," said the Flopglopple. "I like your company."

E.T. looked again at the forest, and felt beyond the forest to the gardens, the flowers, the blooms. Once we take this ship, E.T. will not phone home. The call will not be accepted.

He put his foot out, and took a step.

"For Elliott."

His heart-light flickered, and from it a ray of the highest order shot forth, indicating sacrifice for love. It traveled to the heart of the universe, which is everywhere, and was duly noted—but E.T. knew nothing of this, only felt terrible guilt and despair in his aged soul.

"Look at it," said Micron, staring at the huge,

sleeping installation. "And it's all mine to play with—every last di-nerkling, gam-axiter, and resiston." He stretched himself to his full height, of approximately thirty centimeters, depending on whether or not he was wearing his padded socks. "I've always wanted a puzzle like this to play with."

"Everyone's asleep?" asked the Flopglopple.

"Yes," said E.T.

"Then I'm going to race down," said the Flopglopple, and sped off, stirring leaves and dust in a whirl. In a moment, he was skidding to a stop among the runway lights. "My first inclination," he said to himself, "is to run amok. But this is a serious operation—" He looked up the hill, where Sinistro was leading the hijack party toward the pad. "—and so, I'd better behave, as well as I can, which is a borderline phenomenon, at best."

He ran into the dining hall, where all the Micro Techs and Mind Holders were snoring at their tables. "Asleep in the soup," said the Flopglopple. He lifted up the head of a Micro Tech; noodles were attached to the pugnacious little nose, and bits of vegetable covered the technically minded brow. The Tech's wide lemur-like eyes fluttered. "Too many volts across the sleep-fuse, causing it to blow," observed the Flopglopple. He dropped the head back into the bowl.

He looked at the table of the more evolved Mind Holders. "Their sleeping forms become embryos," he noted. The shapes of the Mind Holders had curled and distended like tadpoles, into great heads and tiny appendages.

"Big dreams, profound ones, flow through the Mind Holders as they doze," remarked the Flopglopple, and at this moment he might have thoughtfully put a toe in his ear, but E.T. was entering the hall and calling for him.

"Coming," said the Flopglopple, speeding through the aisles.

E.T. looked around at the spectacle of the drugged launch staff, snoring in their bowls. "Wasted," he said to the Flopglopple. "I've wasted the entire crew, and every single technician. I, who'd never hurt a fly, have just rendered two hundred individuals unconscious."

"With their elbows in the salad," said the Flopglopple.

"However—" E.T. motioned him back toward the door. "—we have no time for talk."

They stepped back outside and joined the other hijackers, who were hurrying toward the ship. But the Flopglopple stopped suddenly, and turned to E.T. "Someone is awake."

E.T. felt it at the same moment, a beam of consciousness from close by.

Two old botanists like himself stepped through the hatchway of the ship, where they'd dined alone in the Botanical Wing. Now they gazed in disbelief at the dark metallic creatures of the past, who were charging toward them.

The botanists were unaccustomed to violent actions on their own planet, but they saw that their beloved ship, with all its botanical specimens, was in danger. Their protective instinct sent them down the gangplank to defend against the dark lords.

A sound like humming wires came from Sinistro, Occulta, and Electrum, and the old botanists were repelled in a backward somersault by the magnetic field the dark lords had thrown up around themselves—a shield they could project to a great distance.

E.T. stared aghast as his fellow botanists bounced on their heads, eyes rolling about in terror. Their glance met E.T.'s and they questioned him.

"Is this by your order, dear colleague? Are we dreaming?"

"No," said E.T., "I am the dreamer, a foolish one. Forgive me."

He tried to show them his heart-light, but it wouldn't go on, and theirs were hidden too, by fear. They continued to gaze at him, unable to comprehend the emotions sweeping the launch pad.

"An ancient wind," said one of them, "has returned to ravish the night."

"I'm just borrowing a spaceship," said E.T.

Sinistro's armor plate opened, a long finger extended, and a stream of energy shot from it, forming itself in a magnetic coil around the two botanists and imprisoning them. Repelling their attempts to grip it, it kept them bound to the center of the magnetic field.

The two botanists sat in their whirring magnetic prison, and stared in disbelief at E.T., their minds still unable to comprehend this display of violence. "No one," said one of them softly, "has been forcibly restrained on this planet since—the last beginning, ages ago."

"Harmony, peace, and light," croaked the other toward E.T.

"Locking people in a cage," joined in the first one, "is the act of a barbarian."

"If we are caged, if cages are in order for botanists, why aren't you in a cage too?"

E.T. gazed at them. "My cage is different," he said

with a groan, and stumbled around the starcruiser. Deep disorder was filling his mind, and he swayed unsteadily, bumping into guy wires and landing struts.

"What's wrong with him?" asked Sinistro.

"The enormity of his actions has staggered him," said the Flopglopple. "The higher centers of his brain refuse to commit themselves to the night's activity."

"I am a vegetable in the frost," said E.T., his voice trembling. "Injured, spoiling inside . . ."

"We board," said Sinistro, pushing past E.T. Electrum and Occulta joined him at the gangplank. They started up the stairs. Suddenly Sinistro was flipped backward through the air, as he had flipped the old botanists, and Electrum and Occulta came tumbling after him.

"The cruiser," said the Flopglopple, "is ringed with a faint glow."

Sinistro was hurling himself against it again, only to be hurled back down the gangplank, his armor plate clattering. Tumbling along the ground, he came to rest at Micron's feet. He looked up, his head and mirror eyes flashing with anger.

"A repulsor field. We've got to defuse it. Quick, you. The blockhouse!" He pointed at the Ground Control Station, and Micron obeyed, and raced toward it.

"The ships of Lucidulum are alive," he muttered to himself as he flung open the door and entered the command post, where the ship's remote control system was housed.

It was a Micro Tech's dream, and he bounced up and down with excitement. "Yes, everything is here, the heart and mind of the ship. Well, *there's* a messy circuit." He saw an area, presently under repair, a wire dangling from a control panel. He shook his head in dismay. "How can they run a launch pad with such sloppiness?"

True to his Micro compulsiveness, he quickly finished the repair of the panel, for he hated to work in a messy environment. Another inefficient corner caught his eye, the cruiser's remote control music center also under repair. *"That* will have to be repaired at once. I can't make a flight without music, it's unthinkable."

Sinistro burst through the door, head flashing. "What are you doing?"

"Fixing the music center."

"The *music* center? You little idiot. Get busy!"

"I refuse to be hurried."

Sinistro dragged him to the center of the room. "Quickly! Where's the Repulsor Control?"

Micron studied the wall before them—a solid mass of switches, buttons, and screens. "It's right—here." He reached up to the Repulsor Control and the next thing he knew he was bouncing off the far wall and crashing to the floor with a little *splat,* repulsed by the Repulsor Control itself. "The switch is . . . protected too."

His mind shifted, into its higher logic, Master Tech, and with this mode of comprehension he studied the Control. "You really have to admire what they've done here, it's quite impressive."

"Impressive? You malfunctioning little diode! We're committing a planetary crime of incalculable offense!"

Micron picked himself up slowly, eyes on the wall of controls, mind still in higher logic and unable to receive Sinistro's emotional wave length in his brain. He did receive, quite suddenly, a kick in the pants, as the dark lord booted him closer to the controls.

"Now!" A laser pistol appeared in Sinistro's hand. "Or I shoot."

Micron stared at the gigantic display before him, his wonder absorbing all his motility.

"Beyond comprehension. A life-endowed mode. I'd always thought it was an exaggeration, a way of describing its power. But—" He looked at Sinistro. "—it *is* alive. It's moving the Repulsor Program right now, hiding it deeper and deeper. See that readout there?" He pointed to a screen. "It shows only that the program is moving, but not where. And with each move you make, it reads your intent and moves ahead of you. I must say it's a new one on me."

Sinistro stared helplessly at the board for a moment, and rushed back outside, in time to see Electrum and Occulta rushing the gangplank again. Upon reaching the top, their figures shuddered suddenly, as if they'd struck an invisible wall of bricks. Following which, they were pitched backward in the air, and landed in a heap on the ground, armor muddy and draped ingloriously over their heads.

"We burn our way through," said Sinistro. "We'll repair damage later."

He raised his laser gun and closed his finger on the trigger. A devastation beam emerged. At the same time the Repulsor Field of the starcruiser converged into a brilliant shield, which, like Sinistro's eyes, reflected all that approached it. The devastation beam was turned back toward Lord Sinistro, and sent him diving for cover, face down in profound embarrassment. His armor petals flopped over his head and he looked like an umbrella that had been blown inside out.

Electrum put his bullet head down and prepared to ram the ship. A powerful charge gathered in his body and, like some maddened toadstool, he raced up the gangplank. He collided with the Repulsor Shield, which showed no sign of feeling his attack. He, however, was deeply stunned, and wavered back and forth, his umbos temporarily flattened and throbbing terribly.

Then, from within the ship came an ominous purring sound, and a gunport opened. E.T. stood beside the gangplank, trembling. He'd never known such armament existed on the ship. Now, like a dark mouth, it seemed to grin coldly at them, and E.T. knew that the engineers of Lucidulum had foreseen all emergencies, including those of ancient violence.

"Go ahead, fire!" Sinistro shouted at the gunport. "If I cannot mine the stars, I might as well mine my grave." And he straightened himself for the blast.

"No, no," cried E.T.

The gunport fired. A crackling stream of high intensity light shot forth, and like a spinning lariat, encircled Sinistro, Occulta, and Electrum, imprisoning them as they had imprisoned the botanists.

E.T. gazed in awe at the blazing cage, in which the dark lords raged, angrily opening and closing the petals of their armor.

It has mirrored their own actions, thought E.T., and he felt the higher mind of Lucidulum at work.

"Let us out! Kill us, but spare us this indignity!" cried Electrum, thumping up and down and rubbing his bruised, misshapen umbos. Sinistro, still resembling a blown-out umbrella, was bending his ribs back into place. And Occulta, whose mummy shroud once made him as fearful as some specter of the dead, was slumped on the ground, looking like a cheap, unraveled cigar.

The gunport closed, like a softly smiling mouth.

E.T. stared at the ship, wondering what mirror it would hold up to him?

Ignorance, darkness, blindness, stupidity, nescience, incapacity, incomprehension, inexperience, illiteracy, unenlightenment, benightedness, unconsciousness, misunderstanding, and misapprehension, said a voice traveling from the ship to him.

He lowered his head, and a sob broke inside him. Then he felt a frantic little hand tugging at his leg.

"Come on!" Micron was bouncing up and down nervously. "Let's get out of here before we're caught!"

E.T. pointed at Sinistro, Occulta, and Electrum, who were still raging in their cage, shaking their fists and growling angrily at the ship. "I can't leave them," said E.T.

"Why not?" asked Micron in true Micro Tech fashion.

"Because they will be charged with a crime that is my doing." E.T. sat down with a little *plop*. "I must now go soak my head."

"Where?"

"It is just an expression."

"Well," said Micron, "it seems pointless for me to remain here. I'll be more useful elsewhere. And so—"

He took one quick step, a beam of light shot from the gunport, encircled his foot and held him precisely where he was, as the horizon suddenly filled with ships from the fleet of Lucidulum.

The white cube surrounded E.T. He stood in place, looking at the blank wall. There was a sudden stirring behind it, the wall opened, and the interrogation machine rolled out on its little silver wheels. Its ocular extensions bent to and fro, examining E.T. more closely. Its high-fidelity speaker sounded. "You again! What have you to say for yourself this time?"

E.T. looked shamefacedly at the interrogation machine. "I've gone to the dog," he said, from his grab-bag of half-comprehended Earth expressions.

"I beg your pardon?"

"I've been trash-canned. Dumped."

The machine was silent, but its head lights blinked

in an erratic pattern, as if a translation was being attempted within. A buzzer sounded, changing the machine's circuit, and its speaker sounded again. "You attempted to steal a grand starship of the fleet of Lucidulum. Why?"

"To see a friend."

"To see a *friend?* Are you mad? A ship of immeasurable power and beauty, equipped for navigation to the ends of time? You take it, to see a friend? As if it were a bus?"

"My friend lives at the end of time." E.T. looked into one of the ocular orbs as it swayed before him. Then the speakers rumbled, spoke again:

"You drugged the entire staff of a launch base. Some of them are still in bed. You tempted the metallic lords of the underworld into the day and rekindled the greed in their souls. And—you corrupted a Flopglopple." The interrogation machine rolled around angrily, then reversed direction, turning on E.T. "We've had nothing like this in the last ten centuries. What do you have to say about *that?*"

"Far out."

"Far out? Out where?" The machine spun around, bumped into the wall, spun back again.

"An Earth expression." E.T. twiddled his long toes nervously.

The machine rolled under his nose, sputtering to itself. "You no longer speak the sublime and perfectly evolved language of the planet, which even I, a programmed machine, can speak. You have changed. Your flow is no longer that of the Higher Mind. What is wrong with you?"

"I'm—I'm—" E.T. struggled. "—a fathead."

The sides of the interrogation machine opened and

a calipers came forth; it elongated, measuring E.T.'s brow. "Your head is not fat. It is of the correct size." The calipers were withdrawn and the machine rolled away, hit the wall again, and rolled back. "I repeat—what is wrong with you?"

E.T. struggled within himself. He was a master of interstellar philosophy, a Doctor of Botany, a learned, differentiated, higher being. He must give an answer commensurate with the depth of his wisdom. The machine's ocular orbs bent over him and the speakers sounded. "Well? What is wrong with you?"

"I've—flipped my lid."

The machine looked around, orbs twisting. "I see nothing flipped, nor flipping. Answer my question."

"Discombobulated. Lobotomized. Out of it."

The machine started whirring internally, trying to translate. It sputtered again, blew a fuse, and fell silent—motionless and short circuited.

"Wasted," said E.T., touching it gently.

*   *   *

"Ah," said the Flopglopple, "the chamber of Botanicus."

It was a place he liked immensely. The chamber was a golden-hued gourd framed by two pillars of sculpted vegetable marrow, marbled with veins of living membrane.

"You must behave yourself," said E.T., as they walked beneath the arch of gnarled vines.

"Ancient vintage," said the Flopglopple, gazing at the woven twists and turns of the hoary old wood of the arch. From within the vines, tiny lizards poked their heads out and scrutinized the Flopglopple suspiciously.

E.T. led the way, through the arch and into the hall.

"Fluorescents," said the Flopglopple, looking at the glowing petals of the luminous flowers that lined the hall. When E.T. wasn't looking, he quietly plucked a few of the petals and surreptitiously swallowed them. A moment later his toenails lit up, most conspicuously. He quickly hid them in the moss carpet that covered the hall, a ruby-colored mat edged with amber fringe. "Its softness and beauty are unequaled," he said nervously, digging his toes in.

E.T. nodded dully. The luxurious pattern of the carpet, its smooth silken texture and the lovely pattern of the moss, as well as the Flopglopple's glowing toenails, were lost on him. He was sunk in gloom and regret.

"Can I cheer you up?" asked the Flopglopple.

"There's only one thing in the universe that might comfort me now."

"Your Flopglopple hanging around your neck?" The Flopglopple poised himself for the move.

"No," said E.T. "It is small, round, and brightly colored, the treasure of time and space."

"Is it a pellet of deuterium for propelling a spacecraft?"

"It is Reese's Pieces."

The Flopglopple scratched his head with his glowing toe. "And where do you get it?"

"Elliott alone can supply it."

E.T. stepped through the next doorway, to the innermost part of the chamber. There Botanicus sat, in a chair woven of vines and flowers. Little lizards were seated on the arms, basking in his thought, and the flowers themselves were all turned tropistically toward him, as if he were their source of light. E.T. shuffled forward, his step mired in failure; his creased old fingers trailed limply along the floor.

Botanicus leaned forward in his chair of living green. "Demoted again." He shook his head and said, "You cannot steal the fire of the Fleet. Not only is it forbidden, it is impossible."

"What am I to do then?" asked E.T.

"Ponder another solution."

"My solution is far, far away, beyond the Ocean of Lights." E.T. rubbed his brow with his leathery hand. "My head holds many whispers from Earth. My heart holds a feeling. I am bound to Earth, and to Elliott, forever."

Botanicus leaned back in his chair, leaves folding themselves around his head. "My fields hold many secrets."

The walls of the chamber of Botanicus were tapestries of living blossoms, day-and-night blooming. He rose from his chair and walked to one of these tapestries, whose design was concentric circles of flowers, their stems all intertwined. He touched a leaf, adjusted a petal. "My fields hold many secrets," he repeated, as if to himself.

E.T. knew the interview was at an end, but the Flopglopple had the strangest feeling, of something known by him, yet lost in the trails of time. He backed out of the chamber, eyes still on Botanicus, and on the tapestry of blossoms. "What feelings are these?" the Flopglopple asked himself, as a little ripple passed through him, of a dream not yet dreamt and yet having the trace of a thing so old—of a plant, one plant, so old, so powerful—and very important to his beloved friend.

He looked at E.T. "Many moments of my long life seem to be converging, around a nebulous center."

"Why are your toenails glowing?" asked E.T., and then, looking at the Fluorescents and discerning a few broken petals, he knew why. "You've not behaved!"

"But—but—but—" The Flopglopple tried to stammer out the feeling, of just what E.T.'s solution was. *I almost have it, but because of my unpredictable and flamboyant nature it keeps escaping me. But I'll come up with it.*

Then, seeing the lizards in the arching arbor, he tried to catch one, and in his chase down the path he forgot about the almost-perceived solution to his friend's problem because chasing a lizard is so all-engrossing.

E.T. took the other fork of the path, which was bordered with pointed crystals pointing to the sky. The charge within them would build until it drew thunderhead storm clouds, and give rain to Botanicus's central garden. Attending to these crystals were a number of apprentice botanists, youngsters who shied away from him now—for his attempt to borrow a starship was common knowledge and they were reluctant to be seen with him or to suffer from his influence.

The Flopglopple, feeling this insult to his friend, came racing back to E.T.'s side. "Don't pay any attention," he said.

"I shall handle myself with perfect dignity," answered E.T. He elongated his neck to the extreme, until his head was towering; then he put his thumbs in his ears and waved his fingers at the young botanists, who drew back in shock.

"That's wonderful!" cried the Flopglopple, immediately imitating it.

"I learned it from Gertie," said E.T. He continued staring defiantly at the young botanists, and added, "Give me a break."

Then he walked on, lowering his neck and twiddling his thumbs behind his back. "These youngsters, only five-hundred years old—"

"Yes," said the Flopglopple, putting his own thumbs behind his back and twiddling them. "They think they know what life is all about."

"But one day," said E.T., "they may find temptation in *their* path, and be *kerflummoxed.*"

"Kerflummoxed?"

"An Earth word," said E.T. "They say things so perfectly there. And if I continue to study like a real Drop Out, one day I will master the language. I will be able to talk to anyone on Earth—to mathematicians, astronauts, lawmakers, botanists, and—and *nerds.*"

"Nerds?"

"They are a small but important group. Elliott said there is always one in every neighborhood." E.T. extended his arms, to show the Flopglopple how he would speak to an Earth gathering. "Ladies, gentlemen, nerds, good afternoon. I come from the stars to greet you."

"Inspired," said the Flopglopple, clapping.

"With practice I'll have every nuance of the language at my command and will be able to fan the breeze like a real numbhead."

"I'm certain of it," nodded the Flopglopple.

"But," said E.T., "if we never get to Earth, what

good will my mastery of fanning the breezes do? How will I ever help El-li-ott?"

His voice died on the wind, but his inner feeling went beyond the atmosphere, and crossed the airless gulfs of space, descending to Earth in a parking lot, where the attendant ran over it while backing a customer's fender into a wall. ". . . got 'er, she fits snug . . ."

The tiny bit of telepathy, a miniature of E.T., picked itself up and brushed itself off. It looked around, trying to figure out where it was, as the attendant bore down on it in a new Mercedes, whose clutch he was destroying.

El-li-ott, said the little telepathic entity, as it was struck by the Mercedes and sent flying across town.

It landed on the high school football field, where it felt a familiar vibration. It was emanating from Elliott's brother, Michael. Tryouts for the varsity team were in progress, and the coach was watching Michael from the sidelines, trying to decide whether or not he was varsity material. He turned to his assistant, who had just warmed himself in the locker room with a swig from a bottle marked *liniment.*

"Whattya think of him?" asked the coach, pointing toward the kicking tee, where Michael was placing the football.

"Naw, he's a washout," said the assistant. "No lift in his kick . . . *kiccup . . .*" The assistant turned away, covering his mouth.

"Munsterweich, have you been tapping the rubbing alcohol again?"

"Naw, my sandwich went down the wrong way." Munsterweich faced back toward the field, where Michael was nervously getting ready to kick off. "He's not first-string material," said Munsterweich.

"It's all in the toes." Munsterweich gave a brief demonstration of his own kicking style, with a slow motion move toward an imaginary football, pretending it was his wife's Chihuahua. "The kid don't have it. No *punch* in his kick."

Michael was standing in place now, looking left and right at his teammates as they lined up, awaiting his boot. A few yards ahead of them, E.T.'s telepathic form had found its way to the kicking tee, and had climbed onto the football, for it saw that Michael was very attached to it, and at this very moment considered it the most important object in the world.

". . . no *wallop* on his follow-through . . ."

The signal was called and Michael ran toward the ball, praying that he'd get a good one off, for if he didn't show something today, his name would not be posted on the tryout list tomorrow. It was his last year of school, and a place on the team meant everything to him. Please, he prayed, please, please, please . . .

". . . timin' . . . all a matter of timin' . . ." observed Munsterweich as he reflected on the fact that it was time for some more liniment on his gums.

The players moved with Michael, and E.T.'s little telepathic self observed that Michael needed to relax, needed to do something special with all body parts coordinated for one split second, during which the full internal power-thrust could manifest. A double beam of mental equilibrium shot forth from the tel-entity, and hit Michael in the knees, from which it spiraled through his body, adjusting each joint and muscle in a single perfect flex, as Michael brought his arcing foot to the ball.

". . . hasn't got any dynamite in his kick . . . *kiccup* . . ."

KA-BLAMMMMMMM

"Munsterweich, look at that kick! Look!"

The ball was lifting at spaceship velocity and hurtling down field, over the heads of the two waiting receivers, over the goalposts and out over the stone wall surrounding the stadium, where it disappeared from view.

"Put that boy's name on the first team roster, Munsterweich."

*   *   *

E.T. and the Flopglopple sat in the ornamental gardens of Botanicus. The garden was art, mathematics, and botany. The beds were arranged in subtle geometric forms: flower ellipses, and spiraling cones of floral design climbing overhead; expanding octahedrons of transparent plant membrane.

"A sense of infinite peripheries," said the Flopglopple.

"A flower is the geometry of the universe," answered E.T.

They stared at the teacher's displays—vines in parabola suggesting tunnels to other dimensions. "Central gold buds," said the Flopglopple, peering into one of the garden displays. "The functioning inner infinitudes."

"Many a student has wandered here," said E.T. He nodded toward floral transformation rays, that made the eye believe it had come to a place beyond measure, to a plane of hedgerows infinite in extent. "But we mustn't tarry," said E.T., and he led the Flopglopple away, though his thoughts continued out loud as they walked. "Only the foremost students can solve the riddles of Botanicus."

The Flopglopple reflected on this, then spoke. "He gave *you* one of his riddles just now in his chamber."

"No, he was only talking," said E.T. "I should know, for once I was his foremost student."

"A riddle . . . most important . . ." The Flopglopple had his toe in his ear, trying to understand it. *My fields hold many secrets.*

E.T. smacked his fist into his wrinkled palm. "I must retrieve my high intelligence, my great awareness, my cosmic scope. Then, should I ever return to Earth, I will be a real—doubleheader."

"The advanced students on Earth have two heads?"

E.T. didn't hear. "After all, I'm a Doctor of Botany. This signifies that my mind has become a high-power source, able to make profound leaps. I'm a mental athlete, a real—how did Elliott call it—a real *jockstrap.*"

The Flopglopple stared at him, awaiting an explanation, but E.T. had fallen into deep reflection, on the most advanced theories of plant growth, his speciality.

He wandered on thoughtfully, out of the gardens of Botanicus and onto a path leading to the forest. The Flopglopple followed, and observed the faint aura shining around E.T.'s body, and remarked, "This is the doctor of old, pondering the mysterious." And he observed that leaves were unfolding from their silent centers as E.T. passed. "Drawn by his concentration," said the Flopglopple.

Tiny lizards came out upon the leaves, to listen to the Doctor of Botany's thought. E.T., absorbed in himself, began to think out loud.

". . . energy, mass, paradox of the plant. Innermost seed, infinitude of the compressed . . ."

The lizards nodded, following his words closely.

"...open soil of the Parent Ground...seed transfer...drop one's cookies, doing diddly-bop."

The lizards looked at each other, frowning. *What did he say?*

I don't know. Sounded like a new incantation.

Truly, he has traveled and learned.

E.T. walked on, hands behind his back, webbed feet shuffling slowly, still talking to himself. "...then the crystals of lightning flash. The seed rejoices in itself, holding a universe within, preparing to be born. Soon the seed will make the scene at Fat City."

The lizards twitched their tails nervously, scratching the sound into the ground, as odd images came to them from some place far off. Contemplating these images, they fell back into their leaves and remained there in stillness.

E.T. and the Flopglopple continued on through the wood above the garden. The path turned, along a natural wall of rock, which rose like a dragon's scaly spine out of the ground. It was filled with cracks and fissures, one of which had suddenly claimed the attention of the Flopglopple. "Emanation. Mind from the deep!"

E.T. froze with the Flopglopple, as their subtle mental receivers came on, and they heard dark voices, echoing in the planet's depths and traveling along through subterranean seams, and exiting from the fissure in front of them.

we never got our bicycles

"Sinistro," said the Flopglopple, and he and E.T. fell to their knees in front of the fissure, and listened to the next transmission:

nor our ballfoot helmets

"Electrum," said E.T. softly.

nor our own closet

"Occulta," concluded the Flopglopple.

The sound of the dark voices grew faint, and traveled on, through other veins. "I wish," said E.T., "I could do something for them to make up for all the trouble I caused. They were chastised, stripped of their mining guns and sent back to the depths in disgrace."

"I'm always in disgrace," said the Flopglopple. "It has its advantages."

"Those poor old miners," said E.T. "They were good company, if a little impetuous. And what did they get from me?"

"The shaft," said the Flopglopple.

"I'll make it up to them somehow. After I get myself out of the House of Dogs. For that is what I am in, once again. But do you know something?"

"What?"

"I don't give a fudge."

"I am observing a tone of stubborn aggressiveness in your nature, heretofore unknown."

"Life on Earth has given that to me," said E.T.

The Flopglopple followed him, along the stony ledge, and out of the forest, their direction taking them into another part of Botanicus's vast agricultural region. "Where are we going?" asked the Flopglopple.

"Back to the fields," said E.T. He led the way, down into the patchwork of different crops. Each patch was bordered by irrigation ditches, and footbridges crossed at regular intervals.

"No other workers," said the Flopglopple.

"Yes, the area is for us alone. The Court of Lucidulum has ordered that I work with the most difficult plants, to keep me out of trouble."

"Trouble is a thing out of which I've always derived much interesting knowledge," said the Flopglopple.

They started across one of the little footbridges, when a hideous shrieking filled the air and agi Jabi, the scarecrow plant, leapt out at them, waving its arms. E.T. and the Flopglopple wobbled, and fell backward in fright into the irrigation ditch, in nutrient up to their ears.

E.T. gazed at the scarecrow plant, whose bright kernel eyes were glistening. "Must you?" asked E.T.

I must, said agi Jabi, and folded its stalks back into stillness, something like a smile crossing its countenance.

E.T. and the Flopglopple picked themselves out of the ditch and climbed back onto the bridge. E.T. pointed to the garden patch ahead of them. "It contains one of the most difficult plants in the region." He looked back over his shoulder. "Other than agi Jabi."

He led the way into the garden, where row after row of tall, simple-looking plants grew. But no sooner had he started down the first row, than one of the green stalks swung out, forcing him to his knees.

Duck or be struck, said a soft vegetal voice.

Then another of the plants, and another, lashed out their sinewy limbs, and E.T. and the Flopglopple had to move in a crouch through the wildly whipping row, running it as if in a gauntlet.

"The garden of Antum Tadana," said E.T. "It is my punishment."

The tall violent plant, Antum Tadana, continued

whipping its long, sinewy branches back and forth.

"B. good," said E.T.

But one of the branches crept beneath him, grabbed him by the leg and lifted him in the air. He hung there, upside-down.

The Flopglopple addressed the plant: "Antum Tadana, this is why no one wishes to attend to your needs."

They attend to me? It is I, mighty Antum, who attend to them. The only good ideas the Lords of Lucidulum ever had came from me.

And to make this point, Antum Tadana shook E.T. in the air by one foot. E.T. groaned to the Flopglopple. "Don't antagonize him. Flatter him. That is how you handle Antum Tadana."

The Flopglopple nodded, and moved closer to the tall plant. "Antum Tadana, allow me to feed you. Permit me to minister to your great, powerful, wonderful exalted rhizome. Give me five seconds to turn on all your nutrient valves, for you are the true source of all inspiration, here, there, and everywhere. The only good idea anyone ever had came from you. You are the wisest, most vigorous and charming of all plants in the universe."

I like that kind of talk, said Antum Tadana.

His long branches lowered, the tendrils opened, and the plant set E.T. back on the ground.

E.T. joined the Flopglopple, opening the nutrient valves, and whispering quietly, "If the truth be told, Antum Tadana is one of the ingredients used in breakfast cereal."

"I see," said the Flopglopple.

"He must never know," said E.T., and crept to the

next row, mumbling praise and flattery, and Antum Tadana watched, branches folded, basking in the sound of praise of his most high and mighty self, never dreaming he was Tum Tad's Crunch Flakes.

They finished ministering to him, and turned to leave Antum Tadana's patch, but the Flopglopple suddenly paused, thoughtfully. "I can't help feeling there is an answer for you here."

"Yes, a branch in the face," said E.T., and walked on, back over the little footbridge. He led them to the next great square in the garden, from which a sultry perfume emanated.

"But why, with such perfume, are these plants so drab and colorless?" asked the Flopglopple as they entered. He pointed, to the row of tall stalks, folded in upon themselves.

"This is the garden of Magdol, the Sulking Beauty," said E.T. "Her flowers are the most prized in the capitals, but she's a plant who likes to be coaxed."

"How do we do that?"

"We sing to her," said E.T. And he began to croak in his rasping voice, an ancient lullaby of the planet.

> *"Opis nazbeth, shipta-ba'lu*
> *Urumolk, opi majo vashnu . . ."*

The central plant in the row lifted one of her stalks very slowly. *I'm tired of that old junk,* said the Sulking Beauty.

"Her petals are drooping," said the Flopglopple. "Her shoots are bending." He looked at E.T. "She wants a new song."

E.T. pondered, hands clasped behind his back. A new song, a new song . . .

He turned, put out his arms and sang:

> "*Going to Kamsas City*
> *Kamsas City, here I come . . .*"

and snatches of everything else he'd heard on Elliott's Fabulous Fifties album, which he'd played in the closet.

The Flopglopple joined in, and began to dance. E.T. pointed his own toes in a tap step and turned. They linked their arms and did a side-shuffle, elbows out.

"One of her petals is lifting," said the Flopglopple softly.

E.T. nodded, pirouetted, shot his neck up and down, and sang:

> "*Tell me, tell me, tell me,*
> *O, who wrote the Book of Love . . . ?*"

And the Flopglopple spun like a top, raising dust all around him in a dancing whirl, his tripodial feet appearing in rapid succession out of the cloud, and he joined E.T. as they sang:

> "*I've got to know the answer*
> *Was it someone from above . . .*"

Along the row other petals began to lift and E.T. and the Flopglopple redoubled their efforts, singing:

> "*I wonder, wonder who*
> *Who wrote the Book of Love?*"

Magdol's golden fringe appeared, followed by iridescent bands of violet, then luminous greens and dots of red, all on thin swaying stems, like the feathers of a peacock. Row upon row began to unfold in majestic undulation. E.T. and the Flopglopple panted and puffed up and down the rows, tapping, turning, side-shuffling.

> "*A-bop-bop-a-loom-op*
> *A-lop bop boom!*
> *Tutti Frutti au rutti . . .*"

Magdol's garden opened, and the birds and insects gathered, to taste her pollen. Her flowers were immature, and needed sunlight, and E.T. and the Flopglopple kept dancing to keep her open and lure her along.

> "*I've been to the east*
> *I've been to the west*
> *but she's the gal I love the best*
> *Tutti Frutti au rutti . . .*"

The Flopglopple was in ecstasy, for dancing and jumping around were his most cherished pastimes, and to be doing it with his friend, for a good cause, made it a most unusual occurrence, for usually when he was jumping and dancing he got yelled at for breaking something. But this! This was official!

> "*Deep down in Lou'siana, close to New*
> *Orleans,*
> *'Way back up in the woods among the*
> *evergreens,*

> *There stood an old cabin made of earth and
>   wood,*
> *Where lived a country boy named Johnny
>   B. GOODE."*

Another official activity was taking place at that
same moment, in the sky about twenty meters above,
where the Contentment Monitor was passing. Its tiny
cyclone of color paused, and its eye-like orb gazed
down at the garden of Magdol, which was quite un-
expectedly blooming. And strange music was being
sung. The Monitor swept lower and saw that the music
was coming from E.T.

"Thus," reflected the Monitor, "these guttural of-
ferings must be from Earth, which he so recently
visited. But can such a barbarous, war-torn place as
Earth be capable of causing joy in one of our fields?
In the fields of lovely Magdol, the Sulking Beauty?
Why, then, war-mad Earth has something to offer the
cosmos. Most unusual . . ."

And the Contentment Monitor sped on, taking its
observations with it, while E.T. and the Flopglopple
continued to dance and sing.

> *"Go! Johnny Go! Go!*
> *Go! Johnny Go! Go!*
> *Johnny B. GOODE!"*

*   *   *

They dragged themselves out of the fields, after a long
day with all of the problem plants—difficult, temperamental hybrids, including the Brooding Tubers.
"I've been bitten, pinched, pricked, swatted, and

stung," said the Flopglopple. "Just about average for me about this time of day."

E.T. turned toward the Flopglopple; his mind was tormented by something the Court of Lucidulum had said he'd done to this Flopglopple. "They say I corrupted you."

"I'm incorruptible," said the Flopglopple, "owing to my resilient body chemistry." He stretched one of his arms out, and snaked the entire length into a knot at the elbow. Then he pointed back to the gardens they were leaving and said, "Reflect on the words of Botanicus, that's my uncorrupted advice."

"That his fields hold many secrets? But how can plants, however mysterious, help me in traveling to Elliott's planet?"

"We'll grow a stalk," said the Flopglopple, unknotting his arm and throwing it upward; the elastic skin of the creature stretched like a thick, creeping tendril into the sky. "And then—" The other part of him turned under, and somehow clambered up the extended arm. "—we'll climb it."

The Flopglopple floated in the air momentarily, as all old Flopglopples could, having mastered their own gravity by acting out silly nonsense whenever possible.

"Oh, my Flopglopple," said E.T., looking at his friend floating in the air. "You have a pure soul, as once mine was pure. And on Earth, I too learned to float in the air." E.T. attempted an Earth lift-off, but he only crash-landed in the bushes, feet sticking out like the rays of two rising moons.

The Flopglopple descended in a blur, down his own arm, and looked into E.T.'s sad, questioning eyes.

"Don't worry," said the Flopglopple, "I'll think of

something. For even a Flopglopple can have his wise moments, as the proverb says, to which I add—not all thoughts are true, but most of them are useful."

E.T. looked at the bizarre being before him, who, though he'd known him for centuries, never failed to surprise him. "Your enigmatic nature has never been fully understood by anyone, has it," said E.T.

"Not in all the passing ages of the planet," said the Flopglopple with a smile. And a radiant little Igigi Gyrum spun out of the Flopglopple's head and gyrated toward E.T. A mental window opened in E.T.'s brow, and the Gyrum gyrated through, into E.T.'s head. A powerful idea spun through E.T.'s brain cells, speeding across the synapses with the speed of a Flopglopple.

"Flopglopple," said E.T. "You are an excellent friend. And tomorrow we must talk more seriously to Antum Tadana."

"In spite of his bad manners and present position in breakfast food?"

"He is a powerful old plant," said E.T. "His gnarled mind has peered into my problem."

And I too, thought the Flopglopple. I too have peered into your problem. It looks like this:

He tied two of his long limp fingers in a square knot and held them up for E.T. to appreciate.

Long shadows were falling. E.T. and the Flopglopple were sitting on craggly old meteorite pieces buried in the ground a billion years ago. The rays of the sun, called Monshoo, Gigantic Blossom, were shining their last splendid colors of the day. E.T.'s heart-light answered, shining its own ruby rays back at Monshoo as it descended, closing itself within the leaves of evening.

"The others show their hearts too," said the Flopglopple. In the distance, on the surrounding hilltops, more heart-lights were going on, as all the botanists paused to answer the great blossom of the dying sun.

Then it was gone below the horizon, and E.T. gazed at the illusions left in the clouds—of a mountain range. Its peaks and slopes were calling him. But why?

He called to the cloud, as if to hear an echo or an answer. "El-li-ott!"

"LL-EE-UT," said a voice from the shadows.

A soft rocket sound, as of some low-level suspension system, came through the brush of the hillside. Then a shiny round head appeared within the leaves.

"Pulsing optic centers," said the Flopglopple.

A robot glided forward, his belly rockets firing gently, so that he hovered a few feet above the ground. E.T.'s long neck extended to the full length, and the Flopglopple's neck shot forward to within a hair of the iron head. "An old model."

"Yes," said the robot in a clicking voice. "I'm old. But I'm spry."

Four mechanical legs creaked down out of his frame and touched ground, supporting him. He shook one of them off to the side in a little dance step, to show his nimbleness, then shut his hover rockets off. His arms were tentaculiferous. His head, besides containing two pulsing optical centers, was also equipped with other functions. The back of it was a video screen, on which information grids might appear if called for, depending on his programming. Retractable beacon and data-link antennae, now withdrawn, were at his ear points. The entire head was a spherical communications terminal of the older kind, and his age was also apparent in the numerous dents that decorated his chest and backside. His metal tentacles were covered with rust and his joints were squeaking.

"Officially scrapped," he said. "But I have hundreds of years of experience. I analyze and synthesize. And

I'm searching—" He paused, his electric eyes blinking slowly. "—for the truth."

He gestured toward them with one of his metal tentacles. "Can you help me?"

"We can oil your joints," said E.T.

"Most kind of you. Haven't had oiling in ages." The robot looked at his chest. "Could do with some rust-proof paint, as well."

His cylindrical torso was covered in sensors, among them a high-resolution radio meter, an infra-red sounder, and high energy electron detectors. From his back, like the wings of some great bat, a pair of solar panels flapped. Between them, like shoulder blades, were telescopic mirrors, and below that a laser retroreflector—all of it miniaturized and powerful, but covered with the fine patina of mechanical old age.

"May I look at your main battery?" asked E.T.

"Please do." The robot turned and a panel popped open in his back. "It's an excellent model. They don't make them like this anymore. I was built to last."

E.T. peered inside. "Very little corrosion." He closed the panel. "We can fix that."

"Wonderful. For my search for the meaning of things will take me at least—let me see—" A whirring sound came from his head, interrupted by little ripples of static, and then his speaker vibrated once more. "—at least six-hundred more years."

And he sat down, with a soft clunk.

E.T. looked back up at the fading illusions of paths in the sky, and reflected on how fitting it was that it be himself who would be chosen by an outmoded, unbalanced robot. For his circuits are scrambled, thought E.T. Robots were never programmed to search for truth.

"Yes," said the robot, "in six-hundred more years I'll know the answer." He gazed into the sky; random crackling sounds echoed from inside his head, and E.T. knew that his wiring was loose.

"Come along with us," said E.T., and the robot stood with them, and joined their march.

*   *   *

The Micro Tech Club was crowded, and the high strident voices of the Micro crowd filled the room. Technological arguments were in progress, as usual, overheated Micros bouncing up and down; their transparent little bodies turned incandescent, and one of them jumped on the table and had to be restrained by an agi Jabi plant, which was kept for such moments, the green creature leaping from its corner and lifting the Micro Tech in its leafy arms and setting him back on his stool.

The Flopglopple entered the Club, and gyrated across the dance floor, to the foot of the stage. Micron was on it, playing his a'lud, his eyes closed, his little form swaying back and forth to the music.

The Flopglopple didn't want to disturb him with words, which after all, are not music. So he pulled his own nose until it was as long as a flute, and then played a tune on it.

Micron opened his eyes, and the Flopglopple pointed to the door, where E.T. was standing. Micron set his a'lud down, and followed the Flopglopple over to the door. They stepped outside, and there stood the robot.

"Well, well," said Micron, "a vintage model."

"I'm old, but I'm nimble," said the robot, and leapt in the air, attempting to click his heels.

"Bizarre behavior," said Micron. "Needs his board checked." He turned the robot around. "Snap open, please."

"Certainly," said the robot, and his back panel opened.

Micron went inside, his skilled fingers racing over the robot's mind banks. "Hmmmmm, yes, one of the old navigator attendants, isn't that right?"

"Yes," said the robot, "I have logged six trillion, one billion, five million, six-hundred thousand, four-hundred and twenty-three and two-tenths miles."

E.T. stepped closer. "You know how to fly?"

"I contain all the star maps for the greater galactic grid." The robot's spherical head rotated like an owl's, and a miniature constellation pattern appeared on the video screen at the back of his dome. "You are looking at the double star region Nahaz Erdu, called the Pass to Immensity, Gateway of Dimension."

Micron brought his own head out of the robot's interior. "His star charts are all functional." He looked back inside. "He has resistor problems though. Probably warps his reality synthesis. I'll just—"

"No!" The robot jumped away, his back panel closing with a loud bang. "That circuit, with its flaw, has been my path to truth."

"More likely it causes you to lose equilibrium, let me just—"

"Leave him be," said E.T., and thought to himself that flaws in one's nature can nonetheless lead somewhere. Somewhere quite unexpected.

* * *

They took the robot home, changed his nuclear battery, oiled and painted him, and on the following morning he returned with them to the fields, his joints working smoothly as he walked. "I feel like a new machine," he said, flexing his arms. "I will solve the impossible equation $\sqrt{-1}$."

His inner workings clicked and a stream of tape was ejected from a slot above his chin. The Flopglopple tore it off and looked at it. "Wrong."

"Even so," said the robot, and continued to flex his arms happily, and emit joyful beeps.

E.T. walked on ahead through the fields, from plot to plot, and when they came in sight of that plot in which Antum Tadana grew, E.T. felt his thoughts dive deep. And the Flopglopple was beside him saying, "Yes, some part of our answer lies with old Antum, though he is difficult and temperamental."

E.T. led the way over the irrigation canal, across the little bridge, and into Antum's garden.

"Antum Tadana," said E.T., bowing before the long green row, "you are the wisest and most powerful plant in all the world."

A long branch extended from the central plant of the first row.

I cannot deny it.

E.T. motioned to his Flopglopple, that he and the robot should open the nutrient valves. "While I—" He sat down beside the central plant, great-grandparent to all the others.

He stroked the hoary old stalk, and petted the gnarled branches. "I wish to travel, to another world. My answer, I am told, lies here with you."

The ancient plant straightened imperiously. *My true potential has never been tapped.*

"Instruct me," said E.T.

In an innermost chamber of the capital of Lucidulum, whose location and description cannot yet be revealed, a report was made by the Contentment Monitor to one who must be nameless.

"The Doctor of Botany, formerly First Class, now demoted, has gone about his new assignment with enthusiasm."

"No more talk of starships?"

"None. He is, in fact, engaged in independent hybrid experiments, wholly contained to the fields of Botanicus."

"What are these experiments?"

"Simple cross-pollenizations. He seems happy." The Contentment eye blinked. "He has befriended an old robot, who has become devoted to him. The robot is a model we scrapped long ago, and ordinarily we would simply dismantle it, but since the Doctor of Botany has suffered from intense loneliness, my section recommends he be allowed to keep the robot."

"What is the robot's program?"

"I inquired directly of the robot. It said it was searching for truth." The CM's eye crinkled with a smile. "An obvious malfunction, but completely harmless."

"Very well. Your recommendation may stand."

* * *

The Parent gazed at E.T. It was night and only two Lumens shone, above the Parent's head. "You have regained your love for growing things. Is this so?"

"Yes," said E.T. His long toes fidgeted nervously.

"And you have your own greenhouse again? Where you practice your art?"

"I'm developing a new strain of the turnip family. It is a great favorite on Earth."

"I think you'd be wiser to avoid all reference to Earth, my child."

"A momentary lapse," said E.T. "I never think of Earth."

* * *

"El-li-ott..." He lay on his little moss bed, and sent his thought-wave out. It entered Nahaz Erdu, the Pass to Immensity, and jumped dimensions, into the space-time of Earth. The little replicant, a tiny E.T. with heart-light on, came sailing down into a playground, in the middle of a Ping-Pong match, where it was paddled back and forth a number of times.

Ow—ch Ow—ch

It was paddled away, with spin on it, into the playground fence where it hung dejectedly. Elliott was at a crafts table nearby. He'd just finished making a beaded Indian bracelet, which had cost him tremendous concentration and patience. It looked really sharp, with an eagle in the middle of it, wings spread. He slipped it on his wrist and admired it; it definitely gave a *heavy* look to his forearm, which tended to be on the lean side, more precisely like a plucked chicken leg. He'd been pumping iron for months now and the only measurable gains had been when he'd dropped a five pound weight on his toe and it had swelled out through his beach sandals. But this bracelet put him on a whole new level of fitness.

E.T.'s replicant had untangled itself from the fence and was making a desperate leap toward the crafts table. It landed among the loose beads, and with its remaining energy, scrambled the beads into a message, the beads spelling:

E.T. PHONE ELLIOTT

"Hi, Elliott," said Julie, walking in through the playground gate. She was wearing denim shorts with hearts patched on them, and a T-shirt that said *Cupcake* on it. Elliott stood up, hit the crafts table with his knee and sent everything flying, including E.T.'s beaded message.

"What a pretty bracelet," said Julie. "Did you make it?"

"Yeah," said Elliott, as he straightened the crafts table. "It's just something I knocked off. You want it?" he said, as if it were no more than a bubble gum prize, instead of the creation he'd nearly gone blind making.

He slipped it off his wrist and tossed it to her. "I've got to split, see you later."

He made a slow, measured exit, feeling her eyes on him, feeling the warm sun, the gentle breeze, senses alert to everything—except E.T.'s message, which was scattered now, little beads lost on the burning pave.

On the other side of the Pass to Immensity, on the Green Planet in a village gourd, upon a moss bed, E.T. groaned. How could Elliott not hear him?

* * *

The greenhouse, one of thousands that were situated everywhere in the fields of Botanicus, had been swept out by the Flopglopple, and its glass had been cleaned by the robot. E.T. had made the greenhouse functional, opening its nutrient valves and filling the center trough. In it, now flourishing, was a transplant of Antum Tadana.

"This plant," said the robot, looking in at Antum, "he is special?"

"He contains the seed of a great energy," said the Flopglopple as he swept the robot's feet, his own feet, and the feet of the trough.

"And this?"

"That is a Gertie geranium," said E.T. "From a far-off world."

"A most lovely flower," said the robot, as its electron sensor came on. "Of course, I am no judge of such things, but the world that produces this blossom must be an exquisite place."

"We shall make cuttings of it," said E.T. "And increase its loveliness."

The robot moved on to a homely little plant, within which a modest vegetable was beginning to appear. "And this?"

"It is called a turnip," said E.T., "and this is what we are going to do with it—" He showed the Flopglopple and the robot how a hybrid was to be made, between the turnip and vigorous Antum Tadana.

"And what will be the result?" asked the robot.

"A very big and very hard-skinned turnip," said E.T., enigmatically, and began the crossbreeding of the two plants.

* * *

The little turnip sat, mutely brooding on the new activity bred into it; strange un-turnip-like surges were suffusing it, and its outer shell was growing harder than any turnip's ever had before.

Beside the center trough another trough had been placed, now attended by the robot. He hummed mechanically as he weeded and watered, and was most affectionate with the row of little plants in this new trough. They were a rare species, a relative of Yaa Iram the Fire Plant. Each of the plants had a single fruit upon it, whose shell inside and out, was heat resistant. A spiny ring grew around its center. "Don't touch," said the robot, when the Flopglopple came near. "Those spines are charged. They fire into the heart of the fruit."

"It's breathing," said the Flopglopple, pointing to the undulating, mouth-like cavities at each end of the plant.

"It draws igneous gases into itself and digests them with a bang."

The spines crackled with their growing charge, which was suddenly released into the heart of the plant. A muffled roar was heard, and the tenacious roots of the plant had to grip hard to keep it in place, as plasma exhaust came out the back end of the little fruit, along with a single floating seed. "It has dined," said the robot, and moved to the next one, where the process was repeated.

"A most energetic little plant," said the Flopglopple, as the muffled roar was repeated all down the row.

"A remnant of earlier ages," said E.T., "when the planet was nearly molten and the air on fire. It is called Eruca Vara, the Fusion Bloom. It is thought to have once been tremendously powerful, able to withstand four-hundred million degrees of heat. But whatever it breathed at that time has passed out of memory."

"Out of memory," said the Flopglopple. "And yet—"

"Yes?" asked E.T.

"Somewhere—" But the Flopglopple's mind, stretch as it might, could not quite reach the era in which the mysterious power had flourished.

"We shall increase its size, in any case," said E.T. And he opened the nutrient flow to the trough of Fusion Blooms.

Overhead, E.T. and the robot had hung a network of incandescent wire, the wire shaped into glowing quadrangles and octahedrons. "What are these forms?" asked the Flopglopple.

"They are the blueprint of the plant world's desire and design," answered E.T. "Sound waves pulse along these wires and affect the plants below, intensifying their growth harmonics."

The robot was checking the overhead system, running its signal through his electronic brain. A row of lights flickered across his forehead, as he read the current. "Just a bit more amplitude," he said, raising the gain on the hanging device. "The plants will like that, I'm sure."

The Gertie geranium certainly liked it; in fact where there had been one lone geranium in a pot there was now a row of the flowers, brightly blossoming, and E.T. sent the Flopglopple out each day to plant a new cutting somewhere in the fields of the Green Planet, so that Gertie's gift to him might spread everywhere.

Beside the row of geraniums, the row of little Fusion Blooms continued their muffled, explosive breathing, and the turnip wondered inside itself at the odd sensations permeating its cells. If it could have spoken it would have said that it was some turnip indeed.

And then its leaves suddenly turned up at the ends, and its roots began to tingle.

Botanicus entered the greenhouse.

He was accompanied by one of his large lizards, with fast-flicking eyes and tongue. Botanicus's own eyes were sweeping the area quickly, from trough to trough, and to the geometrical stimulators hanging above them. Then his glance found E.T. "A new experiment, Doctor?"

"For a bigger—turnip."

Botanicus stepped over to the pot where the little vegetable was growing. He stroked its surface gently. "With a skin like carbon steel, I see."

"To withstand frost at the polar extremity of our planet," said E.T.

"Where everything is enclosed in weather domes and heated by sun mirrors? But—" Botanicus smiled. "—nonetheless an interesting attempt."

Botanicus pondered, hands locked behind his back, all ten of his fingers glowing with the higher power. His lizard slithered across the floor, cunning eyes seeming to peer through each thing to its soul, but what it did with its knowledge was unknown. The lizards of Botanicus, like the teacher himself, kept their own counsel.

"And the fiery relic?" He stepped to the row of Fusion Blooms, which the robot was tending. The robot's head echoed with clicks and a length of tape emerged from his chin slot, as he said, "Vegetal Energy Experiment Number Five."

"And its application?" asked Botanicus.

"A self-sustained heating unit for use in the aforesaid polar outposts," replied the robot, as he'd been instructed.

Botanicus turned and looked at E.T., their eyes holding each other's for a long while, and E.T. felt the teacher's great mind probing him and discovering all that was hidden in his heart. *He knows what I am trying to create*, thought E.T., *and so it ends*.

Botanicus continued gazing at E.T., and then at the troughs, his head slowly nodding. E.T. knew that in the next moment the order would come to dismantle everything, that the agricultural section could make better use of his talents than in this turnip business. Would a reprimand follow as well? More time in the House of Dogs?

"I strongly recommend," said Botanicus, pointing to the turnip, "that you include the nutrients Lota-120 and Ertong Number 7." He stroked its leaves. "They will add intelligence and elasticity to the walls. And you will want that."

Botanicus smiled and turned to the door, his lizard slithering after him. The reptile whipped its tail, knocking the Flopglopple out of the way, and then it glanced at E.T. He received a sudden jolt of its mentation, swift, elusive, the message sinking to the reptilian centers of his own brain, those beyond his immediate comprehension, and there the message lodged, for future reference.

* * *

"Contentment Monitor approaching," said the robot. "On local Course Zero Two Six, south by southeast..."

The whirling form of the Contentment Monitor streaked from that quarter, over the fields and down to E.T.'s greenhouse, where it whirled around from window to window, and then streamed in through a tiny crack in the door. Its cyclonic body whirled from trough to trough, fanning the leaves of each plant. Then it whirled up to E.T. The fluttering orb studied him carefully, sending its sensitivity beams all over him. "You seem happy, Doctor."

E.T. bent over his turnip, which had now doubled in size. "All is going well."

"A new food, is it?" The Monitor's whirling eye hovered over the iron-skinned vegetable.

"Bred for harsh conditions," said E.T.

"Very good," said the Contentment Monitor. "To be carried to the dead sun regions." It spun over to the robot. "And you, Mechanical Object, are you content?"

The robot's electronic brain clicked and beeped as it bent over the Fusion Blooms. "I search for truth."

Permanent malfunction, noted the Contentment Monitor. *But it's harmless.*

And the Monitor sped away.

*   *   *

The robot's fingers extended, telescoping out with a series of clicks, into a pair of measuring calipers, which it then applied to the turnip. "It has doubled in size once more."

"Time for transplanting," said E.T.

*   *   *

The Flopglopple led the way, out into the forest, where it proceeded to speed around in every possible direction, its great velocity turning it into a blur. "Not here . . . no, not here either. How about over here . . . no, not there . . . let me try . . ."

A peculiar extension had gone out from its ear, long and trumpet-like, which it was holding to the ground as it sped along. Then suddenly it skidded to a stop, listened carefully with its trumpet and raced back to E.T. "I've found the spot."

"A full-force line?"

"Deep and strong," said the Flopglopple.

The robot carried the turnip-trough, his mechanical arms locked against the weight, and his step firm and steady. He'd been feeling much better lately, with the new charge in his battery and good friends to talk with. "I presume we are going to a nodal planting point?"

"Yes," said E.T., "we need the full planetary force. With it, we can grow a prize-winning turnip." He smiled to himself, and a thought-wave went out through his telepathic portal.

The robot saw it go, and quickly calculated its course. "Outer Range Five Zero Five, Gate of Immensity, destination—Earth."

*   *   *

Mary opened the hatch of her broken-down Plymouth, and hauled out the laundry basket, which was piled high with mud-encrusted children's clothing. Her washer was broken and no one had anything to wear. Gertie, carrying a box of soap powder, walked with her toward the door of the laundromat. "But couldn't we fix *our* washing machine?" she asked.

"The repairman is at a rubber hose symposium," said Mary. "His time is limited this week."

She heaved through the door and flopped the basket down in front of the coin-operated machines. "Did you bring the change, honey?"

"Elliott took it all to play Space Invaders."

Mary sighed, took a dollar bill out of her purse and went to the change-making machine. It swallowed her dollar, chewed it thoughtfully, and spit it back out as unsuitable. Mary stared at the machine, then rummaged in her purse again, but all of her dollars were dog-eared.

She walked to the door marked *attendant*, and knocked. No answer came, but water was seeping out from under the door. She pushed it gently open and found the attendant asleep in a large cardboard box. In repose, he had the countenance of a moron, but she supposed he was competent, and wondered if he'd be a good father to Gertie. "Sir—"

He opened one bloodshot eye. "Trouble?"

"Do you have any change?"

"Down the block," he said, pointing dully toward the wall.

Mary gazed at him in his cardboard box, imagining how the box would look in her living room; it seemed more comfortable than her own easy chair, in which Harvey the dog had lately taken to burying his bones.

She walked back out to the change-making machine and carefully pressed a dollar bill against the wall, flattening its edges. Then she put it into the metal mouth. "Eat this or I'll kill you."

. . . course five zero five, destination Earth . . .

E.T.'s telepathic beam, homing in on Mary's vibration, entered through the roof of the laundromat and landed in a dryer, where it was spun around at a high speed.

Gertie, sitting in the laundry basket, looked up. A row of tropical plants hung in the window, and every one of them had just blossomed, petals opening out in a riotous burst of color.

"E.T.!"

The telepathic creature was whirled out of the dryer and spun dizzily through the laundromat; but it sensed Mary's desire, to get something out of a machine on the wall, for she was striking it with an empty soda bottle. "Quarters, you monster, I'm a working woman and I'm tired!"

E.T.'s beam shot into the machine, analyzed its mechanism and tripped it until the thing emptied itself, spilling quarters all over the floor.

"Shhhhhh," said Mary to Gertie, as they quickly scooped up the jackpot.

*　　*　　*

E.T. and the robot joined the Flopglopple in the forest field. "A powerful planetary artery," said the Flopglopple, "runs right through here, and this is its pulse point."

The robot's head swiveled slightly. "Aircraft approaching, southwest, two-hundred-eighty degrees."

"A local cargo ship," said E.T. "We are exposed here."

"But," said the Flopglopple, "our turnip will thrive here as nowhere else."

E.T. nodded, for he could feel the pulse himself, a rhythmic surging that came from just below the surface, as if a giant reptile of energy was passing beneath their feet.

"Very well," he said, as they watched the cargo ship pass out of sight. "We will plant our turnip here. Robot, go back now and fetch our trough of Fusion Blooms, for they must grow beside the turnip. I shall go and see about disguising this place, to keep it safe from passing eyes."

He left the pulse point in the field and entered the forest.

"Where is the Elder Jumpum?" he asked a lizard.

He is with the young ones, teaching them technique. The lizard pointed with its tail, down the forest path.

E.T. walked along until he found the Jumpum Elder, surrounded by little Jumpums who were watching him bounce. As if on a trampoline, he sailed into the air, branches waving. His trunk was light, the wood of the Jumpum noted for that, and his roots, which evolution had made enormously flexible, waved ecstatically in the air. He came down lightly, his canopy of silken leaves and branches acting like a parachute.

As he landed, he perceived E.T.'s presence, and leapt to E.T.'s side. *Jumping time!*

His branches reached out, and he put E.T. into line with the little Jumpums. "My roots are short and weak," said E.T., but he jumped, with all the spring in his legs. His jump did not carry him far, but the Elder was laudatory nonetheless, for he didn't expect anyone but a Jumpum to really know what fancy jumping was all about. *Excellent, excellent, now let's try again.*

E.T. crouched down, curled his long toes and sprang forward. He landed, rolled over in the dust, and picked himself up.

Fine, fine, said the Elder Jumpum. *You're a good sport. Now let's do it again.*

"Elder Jumpum, I'm—wasted." E.T. feebly lifted his hand and then slowly raised himself on one elbow. The Jumpum leaned in over him.

Come, let's jump all over the place. Jumping is wonderful.

"Elder Jumpum," said E.T., "I will jump with you some more, but I need a favor."

Anyone who jumps around with me has only to ask, said the Elder, and he leaned down to listen to E.T.'s request.

*   *   *

"Increasing in size at an alarming rate," said the robot, his calipers telescoped to their full length around the giant turnip.

"It's as big as the greenhouse that once held it,"

said the Flopglopple proudly, for the plant was thriving marvelously in the outdoor spot he'd chosen for it.

"Contentment Monitor approaching," said the robot, withdrawing his calipers, his head swiveling skyward. E.T. signaled with his heart-light, into the forest.

The Elder Jumpum saw the light and called to his family. *Jump to it!*

They bounced out of the forest toward the greenhouse-sized turnip. The bigger Jumpums surrounded it, and the little Jumpums leapt up and clung to its sides. And the Elder Jumpum took a flying leap to the very top of it, as the Contentment Monitor paused overhead and looked down:

"Jumpums jumping for joy. Very contented. Probably holding a jumping contest." It sped off to file its Well-being Report.

*   *   *

"Truly," said the robot, "this is one of the great vegetables." He stroked the sides of the enormous turnip. "But one would need a laser beam to cut through its skin." He turned to E.T. "Is this practical? A demolition team will be required to liberate the edible interior."

"Inject Lota-120," said E.T., and the robot obeyed, needling the growth hormone directly into the pore they'd drilled in the skin of the vegetable. The turnip, enormous now, and realizing it was like no other turnip ever created, drank deeply of the growth accelerator; it knew itself to be indestructible, with skin and roots akin to stone and steel, but it could not surmise its destiny. *I'm one tough turnip,* it reflected to itself, and let it go at that.

Spread out in the field around it were the Fusion Blooms, not nearly so great in size as the turnip, but having increased their heat resistance, through extracts of Fire Plant, their close cousin, which E.T. had fed them. "Good to two-hundred million degrees," said the robot, calculating the strength of their skin and the density of their expirated breath.

"In prehistoric time they floated free," said E.T., "propelled by their own breath. When the planet cooled, they returned to the ground, and rooted. But—" He nodded to their small, straining forms, which seemed, like the Jumpums, to strive for release from the soil with each one of their nuclear breaths.

E.T. lay on the ground, asleep beside his turnip. His dreams were of Elliott, whose dangerous manhood grew nearer with each day. His troubled mind sought to reach Elliott, and a telepathic beam went out.

The robot saw the thought-beam go, and calculated its course. "Five Zero Five again. He has a fondness for the Blue Planet Earth."

* * *

Elliott, Michael, and Gertie sat with Mary at the fast food place, to which they'd dragged her for the evening meal. She fixed Gertie's hamburger and handed it to her.

"Ugh, ketchup," said Gertie, and threw the burger in the trash can.

"Gertie!"

"Well, I don't like ketchup."

"What a terrible waste," said Mary, and contemplated rummaging in the garbage to retrieve the burger, but decided it would be bad for her community image. "Well," she said to Gertie, "you're not getting another one."

"What will I eat?"

"Your green galoshes," said Mary, and settled into the enjoyment of her own lovely Big Burger.

"First game of the season this week, Mom," said Michael. "I'll be kicking off."

"That's wonderful, dear, I assume that's why you need four Big Burgers at a dollar and seventy-five cents each."

They ate their fast food and then her little family dragged her onward into the shopping mall, each one pulling in a different direction. By these tactics they'd tire and confuse her and wind up with all her money. "We're going home, gang," she said.

"Look who's coming, Elliott," said Michael.

Elliott looked down the hall of the crowded mall, and felt a strange sensation pass over him as *she* came into view, her ponytail swinging. "So what," he said, jamming his hands in his pockets.

"Elliott's got a gur-ul friend," sang Gertie.

"He has a perfect right to have one, Gertie," said Mary, as the sudden sinking feeling ran through her, that her baby, her Elliott, was entering the wonderful age of adolescence and would now be unreachable, unmanageable, and unbearable. "She's very pretty, Elliott."

"She's just somebody in my class," said Elliott, his legs turning to soft ice cream as she passed and gave him a sly little smile and a little toss of her ponytail. He pivoted like a windup toy, as she walked on down the hall.

At that moment, E.T.'s little replicant beam came down through the roof of the mall and bonked Elliott right on the conk, and bounced off without touching a single communication nerve—for Elliott was standing still as a statue, staring after the ponytail.

The little tel-entity spun toward Michael, but Michael had turned toward the sporting goods store, looking at hundred dollar jogging shoes in which he must now protect his kicking foot; E.T.'s thought-form bounced off his head, leaving not so much as a ripple inside.

The tel-entity, losing energy, made a desperate rush toward Gertie. But Gertie was looking at the Teen Clothing Store, where she felt she should be shopping; she also thought she should have her own apartment. And E.T.'s beam could not get through even to her, and it spun slowly and sadly in the mall, trying to keep up with the family it loved more than any other in the world.

Mary walked on down the hall ahead of her brood. She stepped out into the cool night air. I feel wonderful after my Big Burger, she told herself. The little E.T. replicant came through the door behind her, its momentum failing. It bumped into a neon sign and sank down to the ground. A carful of crazed shoppers ran over it.

"Owch," said Mary, not really knowing why, and assumed it was her system trying to digest the Big Burger, whose texture frequently resembled recycled cardboard and that, she thought, is probably what they do with all those used paper plates after closing time.

She walked on, and the little replicant sank away, a tiny heart-light flickering weakly in its chest. Then the light went out and the beam dissolved into darkness.

*   *   *

In the shadows outside the Micro Tech base, Micron struck a single note on his a'lud. A moment later a cloaked individual joined him in the shadows. "You brought it?" asked Micron.

"You'll find it in a service vehicle parked in the hills."

"A complete command console?"

"More or less. You'll have to improvise on a few things, but it's a functional system."

"And where did it come from?"

"That is for me alone to know," said the other, who despite his cloak of hiding could only be another Micro Tech, for his stature was diminutive like Micron's, and in spite of the best work of the Contentment Monitor, he was bearing a grudge.

"Very well," said Micron, "then I'm off. And many thanks."

"The pleasure is mine," said the voice within the cloak. "They will learn in Lucidulum not to demote fellows like me." And with these words he moved quickly off.

Micron, for his own part, hurried on toward the hills, his a'lud strung across his back and the night air gently stirring its strings. When he reached the hills, he found the old service vehicle, as promised— the kind the launch bases scrap and recycle every few years, and this one was near that point. But a glance at the cargo area showed an array of electronic equipment in very good shape. And someone would be looking for it tomorrow. "But—" Micron climbed in and fired up the engine. "—they won't find it." Congratulating himself on his cleverness in obtaining it, he lifted the service vehicle aloft and flew away.

"Follow him," said the Micro guard, and a launch security ship entered the air a short distance away.

Micron, flying without lights, sailed over the vast agricultural realm. "I'm a clever sort," he remarked as he flew along. "I move silently and leave no tracks."

"I'm locked with him, sir," said the pilot of the security ship.

"Good," said the Micro commander. "I wonder where the idiot thinks he's going?"

"...making no waves, not a ripple..." Micron touched his controls and banked left. It was then he noticed twin lights following his trackless track.

"Uh-oh." He doubled his thrust, banked again, and went low toward the treetops. The shadows of their branches sped beneath his fuselage. He flipped the aft-scanner on and saw his pursuers dipping with him over the trees. He increased his speed and prayed the old service vehicle wouldn't fly apart at the seams.

The ragged top of the forest blurred, and his grip on the controls sensitized, micronic fingers feeling every part of the ship's performance. Ahead of him, hills leapt into view and he pulled back, soaring over them and then diving back down, into the valley.

His pursuers dove with him and closed. "We can lock him to our hull in a moment, sir."

"Proceed."

Micron shot from the valley, planing again over

the great black forest, moonlight glinting on his swept wingtips. His mind was in the accelerated mode, his head glowing, whorls of thought-maneuver there, matched by his fleeing ship's movements.

His automatic navigator clicked on, code-stimulated from the ground, by one who now guided Micron's ship.

"Course two five evader should do nicely," said the robot, who stood in the forest in a narrow lane of trees, wide enough for one service vehicle. His computer was encoded to match and signal all navigation equipment in the Fleet and most certainly something as simple as an old service vehicle, which was his very own vintage. An electronic beam fired out of his spherical forehead, up the black lane of trees toward the nose of Micron's ship.

Micron felt his landing gear click down, heard number one and two aft engines shut off, and the docking and orientation thrusters firing on as the service vehicle dropped down into the trees.

The pursuit ship tried to drop with it. "Impossible," said the pilot, "I've no room." The forest lane seemed to be dancing, trees hopping about. He yanked back on his controls and sailed upward again, his velocity carrying him over the next chain of hills before he could bank left or right.

When he returned, the entire forest below had changed shape, the forest lane gone, the trees densely grouped. He looked at his commander and shook his head. "We've lost him."

*   *   *

"The sky is clear now," said Micron to E.T. "I've got to get this SV out of here and ditch it."

The equipment he'd brought had been unloaded. E.T. signaled the Jumpums, and a runway opened up again in the forest, trees dancing apart. Micron closed the capsule of his service vehicle and sped off into the dark sky, leaving E.T. to pace nervously about. Their crimes had multiplied again. He'd stolen classified equipment and—

He looked at the dancing trees, who, immediately after Micron's takeoff were forming close-knit camouflage once more.

—he'd corrupted the Jumpums.

*   *   *

The Flopglopple and the robot worked with him, grafting the Fusion Blooms to the circumference of the giant turnip; the tough tendrils of the Fusion were soon circling the turnip, clinging tenaciously to its surface. The Flopglopple addressed the network of tendrils. "See," he said, and tied his two index fingers in a knot. "You must do the same."

The sagacious vine pondered, its rootlets waving freely in the air, and then suddenly their ends curled together in knots, gripping each other. All around the turnip, the Fusion vine met itself, forming an interlocking net.

"Bring the elixir of Tadana," said E.T., and the robot brought a vial of it. E.T. poured a drop in each of the Fusion Blooms and a moment later vitalizing vigor ran through the entire plant; its grip upon itself intensified in a hundred little handshakes of the vine. It tightened all around the turnip and a faint crunching sound was heard as the pressure of its grip upon the turnip was increased a thousandfold.

The mouths of the Fusion Plant now covered the turnip, and breathed gently all around its toughened sphere. The robot gazed at it, his head clicking audibly. "I don't understand, for now it will be all the more difficult to extract the edible center. However, vegetables are not my field."

The Flopglopple stood beside him, trying to get his fingers untied, as he'd made too tight a knot.

* * *

At Base Launch, the head of Security punched up an electronic map. "It is here that the stolen SV disappeared. We recovered it later, abandoned, but this area—" He pointed to the place Micron had landed. "—is probably where the equipment was unloaded. It was a complete command module, and it will not be easy to transport or to hide. We'll fly a recovery mission. And we'll *bring it back*. Is that understood?"

"Will we have assistance from the Lucidulum Fleet, sir?"

The Micro Tech Security Chief drew himself up to his full height, which was about the level of a small waste basket. "We are perfectly capable of handling this."

* * *

A large wooden tub now sat in E.T.'s clearing, and into it the Flopglopple was pouring elixir of Tadana, in large quantities. Standing nearby, in a long line, was an entire family of Jumpums, twiddling their roots impatiently as they waited.

E.T. siphoned a bit of the mixture from the tub, checked its density, and then nodded to the first Jumpum in line. The Jumpum took an enthusiastic jump and landed in the tub, soaking its roots in the vivifying elixir of Tadana.

"Good," said E.T., and waved the first Jumpum out and called for the next. In this way, the entire family of some fifty strong young Jumpums absorbed the potent elixir.

And so it was that the pilot of a low-flying Lucidulum cargo ship was greeted by a Jumpum tree sailing sublimely past his cockpit window, on the arc of a thirty meter jump.

The pilot watched open-mouthed, as the Jumpum descended gracefully downward, branches umbrellaed out, leaves fluttering.

*   *   *

Mary picked up the bowling ball. "Goodness," she said, "it's awfully heavy, isn't it..."

The bowling alley echoed with loud crashes. Alex glanced at her as he wiped his hands on a towel. "But you said you've always enjoyed bowling, Mary."

"Oh, I *do*. I meant the ball feels heavy *tonight,* as compared to the thousands of other nights I've spent here at the alley." She staggered toward the lane, cradling the ball in both hands against her stomach. She took several steps, let the ball fly, and watched it bounce into the gutter, where it slowly wended its way along to the end of the alley and then disappeared with a dull clunk. She looked at Alex. "Sorry."

"Hey, we all blow one now and then," said Alex considerately.

"I'm having an off night."

"You've just guttered a few."

"I've guttered them all, Alex."

"Take a rest," he said, and stepped to the lane with his own ball. His shirt was crisp, his manner calm; his form, of course, was perfect. And she had to admit he *was* terribly attractive, with his dashing black beard and his curly black hair slightly graying at the temples. He'd told her that bowling was important to him, because it was such a complete opposite to computer engineering. "The ball is big, the pins are big, *nothing* is in miniature."

Now he took a few smooth steps and released his ball with easy grace. It went straight down the center, crashed against the pins and sent them flying. She clapped dutifully, but really Alex didn't expect homage to his masculinity. He just needed to knock things around in a violent way in the evening after a long day in the 5 volt Tranzorbs.

And so here they were, bowling.

She found it, in many ways, hard to accept. The last time she'd been bowling was in high school, when one was expected to do such crazy things. The nice part about graduating was that she knew she'd never have to go bowling again. She'd married a man who despised bowling. He'd favored other sports, among them infidelity. So here she was, bowling.

It didn't seem fair.

She turned toward the other part of the alley, where the school kids were playing. Alex came and sat beside her, and followed her gaze. "Isn't that your boy Elliott over there?"

"Yes," said Mary, "a love of bowling runs in our family."

She looked at Elliott, whose face expressed the same misery she was feeling, and the same confusion, for standing beside him was Julie, his little ladyfriend, and it was clear—she was athletic, talented, completely at ease, and she'd dragged him here.

But they were teenagers, doing what teenagers have to do, just as I had to do it.

I just never thought I'd have to do it *again*.

"Ready?" asked Alex, with a patient smile. "You'll find your form on this one."

"Yes," said Mary, "I'm sure I will." Once more she lifted the grotesque ball and lugged it toward the lane. How could people ever do a thing like this for pleasure, that's what she was in the dark about.

She took her position at the head of the lane.

We could be at the ballet. Or the movies. Sitting around in McDonald's would feel so good—she took a painful step forward—compared to this—

I just felt my pants rip.

She watched the ball bounce again, with a life of its own. "It's my—my stride," she said, holding a hand over the seat of her pants.

"Did you pull a muscle?"

"Yes, in my backsi—in my back. A muscle in my back, yes, I think I'd better sit the next one out."

"Are you alright?"

"Of course, it's just an old hockey wound." She slumped back down in the chair. Her eyes returned to Elliott, who was now gazing at the ceiling of the alley, a numb sort of expression on his face. She glanced to where he was looking and saw a peculiar red glow, no more than a pinpoint of light, but very intense. It descended in an erratic way, in among the tenpins.

I'll be right here.

She heard the throaty, croaking voice sounding somewhere in her head. And then Elliott released his ball and it careened down the alley, struck the pins and the little red light, and everything went tumbling.

The voice and the little red light were gone.

"How're you doing?" asked Alex.

"Oh, I'm fine," said Mary. "Just fine."

"I think maybe we should call it quits for tonight. You look a little pale. We can go and grab a bite to eat somewhere."

"But I don't want to deprive you, Alex. I know you need to bowl after a long day of microcycling."

"I'll survive. Come on."

She casually tied her cardigan around her waist, so that it covered the rip in her pants.

They walked together along the aisle, and she liked him a great deal all of a sudden, but she knew she had to be careful with her emotions at such a critical moment as exiting a bowling alley. *What I'm feeling right now could just be the relief you get after ceasing to hit yourself in the head with a hammer. It doesn't have to be love or even affection.*

They passed Elliott's lane, and Elliott waved to her, and she waved back. *And what was that strange look on Elliott's face? Was it Julie's influence? Or— something else?*

A red light flickered above her. She snapped her head back and found herself staring at the neon EXIT sign.

In the interior of Lucidulum, in the veiled chamber, there was consternation. "Jumpums jumping thirty meters in the air? Something peculiar is going on. Isn't this in the area of the demoted Doctor of Botany?"

"I'm afraid so."

"Muster your entire staff of Monitors and *find out what he's doing.*"

*   *   *

The robot watched from his lookout post, from which he could see all of the surrounding terrain. His electronic eyes were riveted upon a spot on a high hill, where another friendly lookout had been posted.

"I sense something is about to happen," said the robot to himself. "My probability mode is on and blinking in my brain."

And in the next second, an agi Jabi Plant appeared on the hilltop, frantically waving its scarecrow arms and giving the warning to E.T.'s camp. The robot read the waving semaphore of the leafy arms and relayed the message to E.T.

"Monitors approaching, southwest, V-formation, considerable numbers."

E.T. and the Flopglopple waved to their family of Jumpums, one of whom still had its roots in the elixir bath. It leapt out dripping, and bounded with the others, who'd already taken their places in a ring— the entire family of trees encircling the turnip.

The Fusion Blooms had by now woven their tenacious weave right into the turnip's skin, fusing their vines to it. But loose tendrils waved freely around the surface.

"Embrace your friends," said the Flopglopple, and the waving tendrils suddenly wrapped themselves around the Jumpums, and bound them to the turnip in an unbreakable grip. The faint crunching of bark sounded through the ranks of the Jumpums.

The voice of the robot crackled again, through a tiny speaker attached to E.T.'s finger. "Monitors entering your area, south by southwest."

The whirling orbs, like a flight of little cyclones, flashed over the horizon. "This is the demoted doctor's sector," said the point Monitor. "Look sharply."

"Now," said E.T. to the Jumpums, whose capillaries were singing with elixir of Tadana. All around the turnip, the attached Jumpums curled their powerful root systems; then they seemed to crouch a little, and then they jumped.

The turnip broke free of the ground, the great vegetable sailing into the air, carried by the Jumpums.

This is jumping, said the Jumpums, bearing the turnip lightly between them, and coming down amidst a number of turnip-shaped boulders with which they blended, as the Monitors sailed by overhead.

Once again, said the Jumpums.

They curled their massive roots under a second time, and sprang into the air again, on a long gliding leap that carried them out over a nearby lake. They floated down, leaves fluttering, and sank beneath its surface.

Immersion, reflected the turnip. *My fate is a mixed one. But I am patient, for something great awaits me.*

When the Monitors landed, E.T. was puttering in an experimental garden he'd created, of forest herbs and fruits, to justify his presence so far from the agricultural fields. The Monitors, their eyes fluttering excitedly, descended around him. "We were told," said the leader, "of Jumpums jumping into the clouds."

"They're high spirited," said E.T.

The Monitors whirled toward the Flopglopple, who had his feet in the tub containing elixir of Tadana. "And what are *you* doing?" asked the leader.

"Tired," said the Flopglopple, pointing into the pans. "Herbal infusion for aching feet."

The robot entered the clearing then, and the Monitors circled him. "Old Machine, what has been going on here?"

The robot's head beeped and whirred. "Gardening detail . . . briiiick . . . I trim and clip . . . as instructed."

"I don't believe him," said one of the Monitors. "Open up your panel."

The robot obeyed, and the Monitor darted inside the robot's back, activating his immediate memory. "And now—give me a readout, Old Machine."

E.T. groaned to himself, for the robot's readout would tell all.

A length of paper was ejected from the robot's mouth, and E.T. groaned again, as the Monitors gathered around it, reading.

"Hmmmmm," said the leader. "Well, it is just as he said. Simple gardening, cutting and planting. Since the machine cannot speak falsely—" The Monitors whirled off as quickly as they'd come, and E.T. looked at the robot.

"A faulty wire," said the robot, raising one finger. "Very handy sometimes when one is questioned."

* * *

The Jumpums emerged in a fountainous burst from the lake, and brought the giant turnip down on the shore among the huge boulders which it so closely resembled. E.T. and the Flopglopple were waiting, and E.T. ordered the Fusion tendrils to release their iron grip on the Jumpums, who stretched and shook their branches out.

"You are good friends," said E.T.

Just some good-natured jumping, said the Jumpums, and jumped off, back toward the forest.

E.T. circled the turnip, inspecting it for damage, but its iron skin was unmarked, and the Fusion Blooms, their own shapes hardened now, were also unscathed.

But his peace of mind did not last long. From

around the edge of the lake, a large lizard approached, and behind it, the figure of Botanicus.

"Watering your turnip, Doctor?" Botanicus slowly circled the giant plant. He touched the edges of the Fusion Blooms that covered the skin, and examined their pulsating petals. "There is a plant," he said, still musing, "whose rhizome is pure lightning. I domesticated it ages ago but finally let it run wild again, as it was so fierce in temperament. Not much is seen of it now, except upon the mountaintops, where the storms gather." He looked at E.T. "Great skill is needed in handling it, for it holds the last vibration of eternity, that force which thrilled the Cosmic Egg in the beginning. I speak of Dagon Sabad, the mountain reed."

He bent down, his glowing fingertips touching a little creeping plant that grew along the water's edge. "Now this is a much different sort of plant, so gentle and cooperative." The glowing finger of Botanicus stroked the leaves of the plant, and its entire system quivered, leaves rustling. He put all the fingers of both his hands upon it, and the plant expanded in a sudden wild tangle, up the sides of E.T.'s turnip. Botanicus patted it, shaping it to the turnip's exterior, and in very little time the turnip was indistinguishable from the surrounding foliage of the forest.

Botanicus turned and gazed toward the distant mountain range. "Dagon Sabad, Doctor. Approach it humbly, and with caution."

Botanicus strolled off, his lizard slithering after him. It turned, casting a last glance at E.T., and in its eyes he saw lightning flash.

The mountain trail was steep and E.T.'s legs were short. Moreover, the region of the mountain was untamed, and it was here that the strangest plants of all were known to grow. Even on the lower slopes, the species known as Nistus Opa, the Illusionist, was at work—from its petals a faint wraith flowing. E.T. looked, and saw Elliott, shaped in mist, waving to him.

"El-li-ott!"

"An illusion," said the Flopglopple, reminding him and tugging him on by. "It reads your dreams and answers them."

The robot had stopped, and was staring into the flower-mist, where he saw an image of a vintage model robot like himself, with opposite polarity, a charming machine, very delicate and winking at him. "...briiick...briiiiz...how do you do," he answered, attempting to kiss its misty hand.

"Come on," said the Flopglopple, tapping the robot on the head with a soft clunk. The robot blinked and looked away from the mist. "A dream?"

"A dream," said the Flopglopple.

"We robots rarely dream, except for short bursts of static. I must say—" He kept turning back as the Flopglopple dragged him on. "—it is a most pleasant activity."

"El-li-ott...El-li—ott..."

The Flopglopple ran back and grabbed E.T. again, prodding him away from the illusion and on up the path.

I alone, reflected the Flopglopple, *am not susceptible to Nistus Opa, for my dreams are hidden, even from myself.*

They climbed on, as the path twisted and turned, higher up the mountain slope. "Who has worn this path down?" asked the robot.

"No one is known to live here," said E.T.

"An odd track," said the robot, "all holes and scratches."

The trail led out of the brush, and narrowed, with rock on one side and a sheer drop on the other. E.T. looked down into the chasm, its bottom lost in shadows. The trail turned a corner in the cliff, and they edged around it.

bounce bounce bounce

They heard it, then saw it—a mountain Jumpum, very light and springy, wildly bouncing toward them on the narrow path, roots up, branches flying.

boing boing boing

It hogged the path, seeing nothing, enjoying itself. Its roots curled under and it sprang straight at them. E.T. searched for a command to stop it, popped into Earth language, muttered "California kiss-off," and dove into the dirt.

The Flopglopple and the robot fell with him, and the mountain Jumpum sailed over them.

"...briiick..."

"...oh, no..."

"...hold tight..."

Sounded like voices back there, thought the mountain Jumpum as it continued down the path. *Must be hearing things.*

bounce bounce bounce

E.T.'s party brushed itself off, and continued cautiously along the path. It opened out once more, into a wide slope. But now the day was ending, and long shadows were falling upon the mountain. And within the shadows were other shadows, of the Fearful Potencies, shape-shifting in black. "They are the Urumolki," said E.T. "They cannot be tamed."

The entities, hooded, black-cloaked, glided by, thin as shadow but awesome, their presence a weight upon the party, as if within their slivered forms tremendous density had gathered. In fact, they were an epidermal organism—thin skin able to absorb nourishment directly through the pores. They were capable of kite-like flight, and their host organism was anyone foolish enough to wander their way. One wrapped itself around E.T. and turned him gently back toward the cliff, as if to lead him over it. Another wrapped itself around the Flopglopple, and spun him too, toward the cliff, for the Urumolki do not like visitors on their mountain.

E.T.'s toes touched the cliff edge, and his warning systems came on, toes tightening their grip. He fought against the shadow, but the Urumolki's weight was against him, tipping him forward.

Beside him teetered the Flopglopple, his tenacious tripod of feet gripping the edge.

The mountain gods reject you, said the Urumolki, and applied their concentrated weight to the impertinent intruders. How dare they seek passage through the sacred shadows of Urumolk. To the bottom with them!

"Buzzzz...cliiiick...beep...that will be quite enough, thank you." The robot's powerful arms reached out to E.T. and the Flopglopple, stripping them of their shadows and snapping the black forms like an old tablecloth. The Urumolki collapsed, into black shapes no bigger than a sparrow's wings. The robot tossed them away in the air, and they vanished in flight. "Must have thought we were cold and needed shawls...cricck...beep...considerate of them, but ...buzzzz...cumbersome things, could trip someone."

"Thank you," said E.T. "We were almost—ding swizzled." He stepped back from the sheer drop, which seemed determined to claim his relatively immortal form.

"Too much hospitality," said the robot, gazing after the fleeing shadows. "Can't do enough for you."

His faulty wire, thought E.T., still feeling the death grip of the Urumolki.

* * *

Night enveloped the mountain. They walked by the light of the robot's eyes, which sent bright twin beams out, through the darkness. His head turned here and there, sweeping the area in front of them. The Flopglopple flopped along beside E.T. "Where does this plant we search for dwell?"

"I don't know," said E.T. "I don't even know what Dagon Sabad looks like. All the texts say is that it must be found at night, for its power to be full."

They picked their way up through slides of stone and low clinging brush. The robot climbed ahead of them, his mechanical hands drilling footholes in the rock; then, from his mid-section a length of climbing rope reeled out. "Grab on."

E.T. wrapped the rope around himself and the robot's inner pulleys cranked him up. The Flopglopple followed, and in this way they scaled the ever steepening slope. "You are a mountaineer," said E.T., as the robot hauled him up the next blank wall of stone.

"Outmoded but agile," said the robot, sending the line back down for the Flopglopple, who hurriedly tied it too low and was hauled upside-down, arms dragging, eyes gazing down into the lights of all they'd left behind, far below.

Their climb had brought them to a smooth plateau, where the Near Moon shone, and E.T. could feel that they'd come closer to it and to those stars he sought, Nahaz Erdu, Gateway of Dimension, which flickered more brightly now, out beyond the dark mountain peak.

The robot's eye beams penetrated the plateau, and caught movement, in the depths of an overhang. A shadow swept out, gigantic, and rose up—a black cape that cloaked the moon.

"Urumolki!" cried E.T.

The Urumolki had massed together, blending their malevolent forms into this great whipping shade, through which the moon's rays could not shine. It hovered above the exploration party, its sinister undulations slowly lowering, a portion of the night itself which belongs to no planet, and is its own ruler.

"Extending hospitality again . . . cliiiiick."

"Run!" cried the Flopglopple.

E.T.'s tongue was tied in fright, but his Earth language finally unloosened, with "Beat it!"

"Very well," said the robot, and ejected a wire rugbeater from the end of his arm as the Urumolki dropped toward E.T., its dark mind a mass of weight and power.

These heights are for the Urumolki only, who alone understand the mountain's magic.

The blanket of black fell on E.T., plunging him in a darkness so dense it was palpable, like a sea of ink. E.T. felt the blackness seeping into his brain, confusing and drowning his consciousness.

"Beating as directed . . . crackle beep . . ."

The menacing shadow snapped in the air, struck like a rug on a clothes line by the robot. "Swift strokes to get the dust out . . . bricccckle . . . breep." The massed shadow of the Urumolki fell to the ground, flattened, itself unconscious now, and there it lay, perfectly still.

"A picnic cloth . . . bleeep . . . apparently that was the intention, to make a nice place on the ground for us. Pity we have no food and a thermos of lubricating oil."

*   *   *

The peak of the mountain was broad, and they stood upon it with the majesty of the constellations above them, calling them on. E.T. gazed at the bowl of stars, and whispered to Elliott, that nothing could separate them, neither distance nor time.

Dark clouds had moved past the moon and the wind had joined them, blowing hard across the mountaintop. Only the light from the robot's eye beams shone, leading the way.

E.T. was searching with his own most sensitive band, feeling in his brow all that moved and dwelt upon the mountain. The power of Dagon Sabad was here, for it was sending out its quiet current, quiet but unlike anything he'd felt before.

"Dormant energy," said the robot, his digital display flashing. "Highest grade."

The Flopglopple suddenly started slithering along the ground, all four-hundred of his spinal vertebrae tingling.

E.T. shuffled around, his toes receiving a vibration of subtle intent. "The mountaintop is its field."

"High molecular activity...beep...nascent... now slightly surging..."

The robot's arms were angled out, receiving the energy flow and computing it inwardly, a length of tape shooting like a serpent's tongue from his chin slot and flapping in the wind.

Lightning flashed in the sky, illuminating the dark clouds and the mountaintop, rock ledges momentarily flooded with a ghostly hue. E.T. felt his mind leap into its cosmic mode, a vision of the aged universe in its beginnings flooding his thought.

The Flopglopple rolled around, vertebrae snapping

ecstatically, as if manipulated by four-hundred electric hands.

The robot's eye beams began a stroboscopic pulsing, intensely bright. ". . . briiiickitttaaa . . . rrrrrrrttt . . . increasing voltage, becoming immeasurable." The top of his head opened and two glowing rods shot out, tips red with incandescence.

The lightning answered, splitting the sky with a jagged tongue of flame. E.T. saw the mountain in its entirety, ash white, a hulking wraith of the night.

And circling above it, caught in the flash, were the ominous shadows of the Urumolki.

"They've forgotten us," said the Flopglopple. "They're assimilating power."

The dark creatures whipped madly in the lightning tongues, a vein-like pattern crackling in their outspread cloak forms. *Homage,* cried their spirits, *homage to Dagon Sabad, who quickened the Cosmic Egg!*

Flaps opened on both sides of the robot's head and four more glowing rods shot out, and electricity began jumping from rod to rod around his head. ". . . rrrrrrkkkkkk . . . zzzzzzzz . . . charging batteries . . . dee—licious."

E.T. continued searching from rock to rock. The mountain was bare, but he'd seen plants growing in stone before, with splendid tenacity. Plants were the masters of the world, from the depths to the heights.

And they liked being talked to.

"Dagon Sabad, who draws lightning from the clouds—" He shuffled along, speaking quietly. The plant would hear, sensitive to the slightest change in vibration. "—Sabad, who stirred the primal atoms, giving birth to the galaxies, and to Reese's Pieces."

The robot clanked along beside E.T., the rods on his head webbed with buzzing light. He held up one metal finger, and the electricity jumped to it, and he drew it out in a line, spiraled it, and wrapped it up his arm in a coil. "...breekle...biiizzz...charge of a lifetime...good for the next six-hundred years."

The Flopglopple snapped along over the ground, a limp lightning-charged noodle, his snaps carrying him to the unseen edge of the cliff, off which he suddenly found himself hanging by two fingers. He extended one of them, elongating it beyond his previous world record, a full five-tenths of a meter, and wrapped it around a jagged pinnacle of rock. He released his other hand from the cliff edge and hung, happily, by just one finger, singing to himself.

E.T. continued his shuffling step. "Dagon Sabad, ruler of all plants, possibly greater than even Antum Tadana—"

Possibly greater?

Lightning splintered the dark, and its downward pointing tip hovered, momentarily sizzling the shadowy tip of a small and nearly invisible shoot of vegetation. And then the lightning seemed to be drawn down, swallowed in the shoot itself.

Antum Tadana would perish here, in a little pile of burnt breakfast flakes.

The plant became silent then, as if returned to its introspection, on cosmic matters, concerning the demise of the present universe and the beginning of the next.

The robot stood beside E.T., eye beams pointed toward the lightning charged reed; his head was wreathed as if with sparklers. "...criiickit...

reeeeep...planetary power source. Directly ahead. Incalculable emission...beyond outmoded computer's power to analyze."

E.T. took a step forward, and felt his toes suddenly freeze, imprisoned in place by a magnetic force rising up through the stones, and the robot froze beside him. "...malfunction in my extremities. Ground grippers locked in the joints. Oiling recommended."

The Flopglopple pulled himself up by his finger and rushed across the mountaintop toward E.T. and the robot, only to find his feet suddenly glued in place and the rest of his body elongating forward and then snapping back like a rubber band.

Thus the exploration party stood, fastened in the stones before the altar of Dagon Sabad, and E.T. knew this power gripping them could hold them for days, nights, weeks, ages.

He leaned toward the shadowy reed in the rock. "I bring greetings from Botanicus."

Ah yes, my foremost student.

"He—that is—I—seek a cutting from your shoot."

Certainly, certainly, said the plant, but E.T. sensed that nothing now was certain.

But his feet were released, the binding power withdrawing back into the stones with a faint hiss. He stepped toward the crevice in the rock, where the shoot was bedded, and the robot shone his eye beams into it.

E.T. reached down to it, and his healing finger glowed, for he must anesthetize the plant first; then with tender care, he broke it off.

A sheet of fire sprang out of it, rising like a geyser, high above the mountain peak. He was knocked backward with the roar, as a fountain of radiance lit the sky, thousands of times brighter than the lights of Lucidulum when a Lord of Wisdom is crowned in primal radiance. This was the planetary crown, rising higher and wider, into a blazing wheel. The heavens shook, and E.T. lay on the ground, trembling in the wake of the surge he had released and seeing his past and the past of the world, and its future dreams undreamt, brooded upon by Dagon Sabad. Systems of flame revolved, as the universe-to-be appeared in shadow form amidst the flames, all of it flowing from the mouth of a plant no bigger than E.T.'s little finger. He whispered his thanks to the mother reed and slowly backed away, the cutting clutched in his hand.

"Stellar magma...blip..." The robot was pointing to the blazing spectacle overhead.

"Come on," said E.T., "let's beat it."

The robot's rugbeater came out.

"No," said E.T., "I mean, we must leave."

As he backed away, his eyes met another surge of light, from the horizon where Lucidulum lay. Intermediate cruisers had blasted off, and were streaking toward the mountain, for its eruption had illuminated the night sky in all directions.

"Hurry," said E.T., though it was he whose legs were shortest and slowest, rocking in little steps across the mountaintop. The Flopglopple and the robot lifted him between them, and hauled him quickly along over the plateau. "Beep beep...maximum acceleration," said the robot.

They sped across the rough peak and dove down a rocky incline as the cruisers of Lucidulum shot by, and circled, round the eruption of Dagon Sabad, whose fiery breath still shot in the air, as if from the heart of a volcano.

"Owch, owch, owch." E.T. tumbled along between the robot and the Flopglopple, but his fingers were still clutched tight around the cutting of Dagon Sabad. The tip was glowing with the brilliance of a diamond, like the wand of a magician in his hand.

Then the mountainside was suddenly lit with enormous search beams from the cruisers, and the robot clicked his own eye beams off, and the Flopglopple fell forward, crying, "I can't see the path!"

Infra-red filters popped on in the robot's eyes, and he took the lead, down the dark turnings of the slope.

The cruisers swept by, beams searching all along the slope. "We must get round that corner before the lights find us." The robot hurried forward, down the narrow ledge, E.T. and the Flopglopple following.

bounce bounce bounce

Roots, branches, leaves came sailing at them, and they flattened out, as the mountain Jumpum bounced blithely over them, on its return journey up the path.

A cruiser beam burst directly ahead of them, and E.T.'s mental receptor felt the brain wave of the crew of the cruiser, certain of capturing someone, possibly a short, unconventional botanist, demoted, First Class.

"Look," said the robot, turning the other way, and pointing, to where the mountain Jumpum was bouncing—a right angle bounce, into a crevice in the cliffside, where it disappeared.

E.T., the robot, and the Flopglopple scrambled after the Jumpum, through a huge fissure in the rock. They heard the Jumpum's bounces echoing down, down, down.

bou-ounce bou-ounce bou-ounce

The robot's bright eye beams clicked on, down a long jagged tunnel in the mountain.

Elliott rode his bike along through the last shadows of the evening. Ordinarily this was the hour he devoted to blowing his allowance at the video arcade, shouting and screaming with Tyler, Greg, and other of his distinguished friends. After which they'd proceed, broke, to a number of interesting street corners and discuss philosophy (girls), their future (girls), sporting events (girls), and the latest movies (girls).

So far, he was the only one among his friends to do more than discuss the subject. He'd actually taken Julie bowling. And tonight he was going to join her in babysitting. Of course, there was nothing really between them. He'd never even kissed her.

He'd thought about it, deeply.

But it wasn't something you rush into.

It required *planning*.

He pedaled along into her neighborhood, and found the house where she was sitting. He rode on by it, indifferently, with his ears burning, his throat tight, and his palms sweating.

He rode to the end of the block and circled beneath the streetlamp. Darkness had fallen now, and his bike cast a long shadow on the pave, then vanished into the blackness as he pedaled out of the light and back up the block. Among the houses ahead of him there was one with the porch light burning.

He steered toward it, hopped off his bike and rolled it into the backyard. He put the kickstand down, settled the bike into place for a quick getaway, and then walked up the back porch steps and scratched like a rat on the door.

He listened as soft footsteps approached from within, and then the door swung open and there she was, looking soft and sweet and beautiful. Her T-shirt said *Pineapple*, and she was wearing faded jeans with red hearts sewn on both pockets.

"Nobody's home, are they?" he asked in a fearful whisper.

"No," said Julie, "they're gone."

The house belonged to the Zontack family, and Mr. Zontack was well-known for throwing baby-sitters' boyfriends out through the side door with a foot implanted in their designer jeans. He was a *large* man, ran a meatpacking plant, and was reputed to have underworld connections, though this was probably a vicious rumor begun by someone he'd kicked out the side door.

"You're sure Mr. Zontack's not gonna check back?"

"No, they went out to dinner and then they'll be going to the movies, so they won't be back for hours." Julie led him toward the living room.

"Ever been here when he—*caught* somebody?"

"Elliott, he's not a policeman."

"Yeah, sure, I was just wondering." Elliott looked around. Front door there, open window here, back door where I just came from.

"Looking for someone?"

"Nice table," he said, running a hand along it as he checked the side door.

"Want to watch TV?"

"Naw, we should keep it quiet, right? So we can hear somebody drive up?"

"You *are* afraid of Mr. Zontack."

"Well, he hung Tyler out a window upside-down."

"That's because Tyler's a creep."

"He was helping to babysit."

"He was raiding the refrigerator."

"I won't go near it," said Elliott, quickly.

"Well, Mrs. Zontack left sandwiches."

"I'm not hungry."

"Elliott, you're so *nervous.*"

"Me? Nervous?" He unknotted his fingers and watched Julie sit down on the couch. She patted the seat alongside her, and opened a book on her lap. "You can help me with my BASIC. You know all about computers."

Elliott took a few hesitant steps toward the couch, and eased himself onto it, leaving a whole cushion between them.

"Can you *see* from there?" asked Julie.

He looked at her smooth skin, and her silky pony-tail. A faint smell of perfume came to him. Julie pushed the book aside. "Well, if you don't *want* to help me—" She leaned over to the hi-fi set and switched it on. The easy listening station was tuned in, and he heard trumpet and violins, playing a slow soft song that went through him in a delicious current from head to heart.

"So how've you been?" he asked. He'd seen her at school just a few hours ago, but it didn't hurt to check.

"Fine," she said quietly, and slipped nearer to him on the couch. "Are you afraid of Mr. Zontack—" She blinked her long lashes. "—or of me?"

The sound of an approaching car stiffened him on the couch. He snapped his head, listening. "Is that him?"

"Who?"

"Mr. Zontack."

"I told you—he's at the movies."

"Maybe he didn't like it. Maybe they walked out." Elliott got up and crept to the window. He pulled the curtain slowly aside, and watched the car roll past through the darkness.

"Other people live around here too, you know," said Julie.

Elliott looked around the living room. On the wall was a picture of Mr. Zontack, with a large shark hanging beside him at the end of a pier. Mr. Zontack appeared to have punched it to death.

"Candy?" asked Julie, opening the box of chocolates on the coffee table.

Elliott took one, chewed it thoughtfully. On top of the TV set was another framed photo of Mr. Zontack, at the amateur arm wrestling championships. It was an action shot, with the veins bulging out of his head.

A victory cup stood beside it.

Another wave of insecurity passed over Elliott, the strange feeling of being in somebody else's house, somebody else's life, with somebody else's baby-sitter. It was alien and unnerving. And then, for no reason at all, he felt E.T., somewhere far away, but signaling him somehow, telling him never to be afraid of anything, to always remember he was connected to the stars.

Elliott opened the curtain again, and saw a flickering red light over the houses, just like the one he'd seen at the bowling alley. It was sailing around confusedly, up and down the block, and then crash-dived into a dish antenna in somebody's yard. Elliott opened the door and ran outside. "E.T.!" he shouted. "E.T.!"

But the light had died out with a little hissing sound, and now the street was silent.

Except for the sound of an approaching automobile.

Elliott leapt into the darkness between the houses and pressed himself against the side of the building. The car slowed, and pulled to a stop, and Mr. Zontack got out, along with Mrs. Zontack.

"So don't take me to the movies," Mrs. Zontack was saying.

"That's right," growled Mr. Zontack, "I won't." He yanked his keys from his pocket and looked around suspiciously. "Somebody's been here."

"Would you please calm down?"

"I can always tell when some young punk comes around. Eating everything in the refrigerator. Snooping."

"Don't you go scaring Julie, you monster."

Elliott crept silently away from the family quarrel,

slipped onto his bike and rolled it out of the backyard. He pushed it past a few houses, then brought it back up through the yards, onto the street, right in front of the dish antenna. "Thank you, E.T.," he said softly, and rode away.

*　　*　　*

E.T.'s headquarters were now in the cave they'd discovered in the mountain. The Jumpum family transported his turnip there, to the mouth of the cave, where it blocked the door, looking like just another vine-covered boulder.

"Security patrols overhead," said the robot, within the cave, his circuits clicking with the contact.

The Flopglopple peeked out past the boulder. The air was indeed alive with Security ships, searching for their lost equipment.

"Nothing but trees down there," said one of the pilots, who would have been interested to know that the missing equipment was clamped firmly inside the roots of those trees.

The Flopglopple watched the patrol fly on over the mountain, and then he turned back into the cave.

The cutting of Dagon Sabad had rooted, spread, and flowered. Lighted by hundreds of Lumens clinging to the cave walls, it now filled many pots. Its leaves were plain and the flowers simple.

It had a marked affinity for the Fusion Blooms, toward which its tendrils crept; most of the Fusions were embedded in the wall of the turnip, but the robot brought one of them in a pot and set it next to Dagon Sabad. The tiny flower of Dagon Sabad quivered and a spark of its sleeping power leapt into the mouth of the Fusion Bloom. The Bloom expanded, a jet of blazing plasma shot from it, and it sailed out of the cave, pot and all, and streaked away.

* * *

"You lost this, Doctor?" Botanicus appeared at the mouth of the cave, the Fusion flowerpot in his gnarled hand.

E.T. gazed at his teacher, trying to fathom his intent, but the eyes of Botanicus were not easily read, their expression like that of the moons, distant, serene, and inscrutable.

Botanicus set the pot down gingerly, and fluffed out the leaves. His lizard crept in behind him, and waddled around the cave, stopping beside the rows of Dagon Sabad. Its eyes closed to slits and its body grew still, as it listened to the internal roaring of the plant, a level lizards are adept at reaching. E.T. himself had heard the roar once or twice lately, sounding deep in his mind, as if Dagon Sabad were rooting there as well as in the row of tiny pots. It was the roar of worlds being born; it was the voice of the cosmic dragon.

Botanicus peered out of the cave door. "A great many Security ships up there," he said, nodding to the sky, where the reconnaissance pattern continued to be flown. He patted the side of the vine-covered turnip at the mouth of the cave. "But you're well hidden. So—" He turned back to E.T. "I shall leave you to your work."

E.T. stepped with him to the mouth of the cave. "Why have you helped me?"

"A culture such as ours, whose evolution is complete, needs a shock now and then. How shall I put it—it needs—"

"—a bug in its ear?"

"Yes, that's it. Exactly. It needs a bug in its ear." Botanicus walked out into the open, but he was visible for no more than a moment, for the entire forest seemed to move to camouflage him as he walked, leaves forming a canopy over his head. *A bug in its ear,* he reflected as he walked. Very handy, these Earth expressions.

* * *

The robot went to a nearby Jumpum tree. "Lift up, please." The Jumpum lifted a long root, revealing the hiding place of a number of high intensity tools. "Thank you." The robot carried a laser torch back to the cave. He pointed it at the turnip. "Kitchen duty. Preparing vegetable."

The thick toughened skin slowly yielded and a door-shaped wedge was cut out of the turnip's face. The robot's metal fingers retracted and were replaced by a pair of pointed digging tools. "Emergency service items. Entrenchment orders, briizz."

And he hollowed out the turnip.

* * *

In the cover of darkness, E.T. stepped outside and examined the surface of the turnip. The Fusion Blooms had now grown deeply into the turnip's flesh, only their petals showing on the surface, from which their warm breath was expelled. He ran his hand over a few of the Blooms, murmuring softly to them, and then went back into the cave.

The door in the turnip faced into the cave, and he circled around to it, and entered the giant vegetable. The robot was at work inside, exposing the inner mouth of the buried Fusion Blooms, thereby connecting inside with outside through the hollow body of the Blooms.

"A most interesting display," said the robot, as he worked. "And they've embedded themselves so symmetrically, as if—they think. And why not?" he asked himself. "If I, an arrangement of wires and chips, can think, can search for something so elusive as truth, why then surely these highly evolved specimens of the highly evolved Green Planet can do as much—can think, and grow, and—"

He paused and looked at the network of breathing mouths his digging tool was gently exposing. "—and much else might they do, these Fusion Blooms of ours."

E.T. turned to his Flopglopple, who was dancing with his shadow in the back of the cave, where a few Lumens burned for him. "Turn and step . . . one two . . ." The Flopglopple reached out, actually embraced and gripped his shadow, hand to hand, as E.T. watched in amazement.

"Flopglopple, you are astounding."

The shadow melted from the Flopglopple's grip, as he seemed to wake in his dancing from some deep spell. "Did you—did you speak?"

"We must now bring Dagon Sabad near to our Fusion Blooms. Rings—" E.T. pointed, indicating that a skeletal sphere within the turnip must be built to support Dagon Sabad.

"What material shall I use for these rings?" asked the Flopglopple.

"Gather the Rakoor Ram, vine of pliable grace. We can shape it here, strengthen it with Antum Tadana and bend it to our needs."

The Flopglopple drew back one leg, poising himself for a streaking dash. A final word from E.T. cautioned him:

"Many search the mountains, hills, and forest for us now. Do not be captured."

"A Flopglopple is not easily overtaken," said the creature and sped off, out into the night.

E.T. stepped from the door of the turnip and walked wearily to the rear of the cave, where he had grown a little fungus bed for himself, and onto which he laid himself with a sigh. "A Flopglopple is not easily overtaken, but a dry old demoted Doctor of Botany, formerly First Class, may not be so difficult a quarry." He sighed again and rolled over. In very little time, exhausted from his labors and his constant hiding, he fell asleep.

His thought-wave switched to the telepathic frequency, and his tele-replicant went out through the mountain cave, and into the universal spaces. It crossed the Pass to Immensity and, piercing the dimensions, came down on Earth, off course by fifteen city blocks, above a midtown pool hall.

"Alrigh', I'll make the t'ree ball in the corner."

"An impossible shot, Fat Freddy."

Fat Freddy knew this, for his game had been falling off lately owing to his being force-fed 120 proof vodka. Vision blurred, cue shaking, he struck the cue ball, just as E.T.'s tiny replicant came spinning down onto it. The added English sent the cue ball in a perfect trajectory, where it sank the three ball.

"Nice shot, Fat Freddy."

I seen some kind of little green guy land on the cue ball, thought Fat Freddy. *I am havin' d.t.'s but it don't appear to affect my game.*

• 216 •

Not *d*.t.'s, Fat Freddy. *E*.T.'s

The little green guy sailed off the cue ball and was on the way again, traveling fifteen city blocks to Elliott's house, where only Harvey the dog was at home, chewing on an old baseball glove.

Not much flavor left in this. I'm in desperate need of a Milk-Bone.

He wandered into the kitchen.

They always make these shelves too high for the average dog.

His paws were up on the counter, his snout straining, but he couldn't reach the box of Milk-Bones, which was plainly visible and precariously balanced.

If we had a canary, I could train him to fly up there.

Harvey lowered his paws, just as E.T.'s little replicant shot in and bounced around from wall to wall.

A little more to the left, said Harvey, directing the bounce.

The replicant landed on the Milk-Bone box, with just enough weight to tip it over, spilling the contents on the floor in the sort of disordered pile appealing to dogs.

Thank you, said Harvey, wading into it, jaws open.

The little E.T. form expired in the cupboard.

*   *   *

The Flopglopple stalked through the woods, with loops of Rakoor Ram over his shoulder; his step was alternately cautious and carefree, according to his nature. "I trust to speed," he said to himself, as he gathered more of the strong pliable vine.

But the forest was filled with Micro Techs, riding in little two-seater pods, very fast and maneuverable.

The Flopglopple watched from the brush as a pair of pods skimmed by, the Security Techs inside them craning their necks around.

"They seem upset about something," remarked the Flopglopple to himself, not knowing that Micro Techs cannot bear to have something of theirs lost, misplaced, unaccounted for, or otherwise out-of-line. That an entire command console, four life-support systems, and an atomic clock had vanished disturbed them to the point of compulsive mania. Their big round eyes were popping from their heads.

The Flopglopple waved to them.

He wondered why.

Probably, he thought, speeding off in a blur, because I'm a Flopglopple.

Following behind him in an equal blur were the Micro pods. Their drivers had signaled to the other pods, a dozen of which were now converging on the Flopglopple, who reflected that when the chase was on, life was sweet.

His tripodial feet churned, his four-hundred vertebrae swiveled, as he tore in and out between the trees. A quick glance over his shoulder showed him the pods matching his wildly winding track. He screeched to a stop, cut directly left and sped off in a new direction.

The pods screeched to the same stop, cut with him, and stayed on his track, only a few meters behind.

"Hmmmmm," observed the Flopglopple, "maybe I should increase my stride." His elastic legs sprang into longer spans, his speed nearly doubled, and again he checked over his shoulder.

The drivers of the pods were shifting gears, pods

streaking into high. But then, throughout the woods, it suddenly became—

Jumping time!

The forest began to move in a dizzying labyrinth, trees leaping every which way, forming chutes, cul-de-sacs, circles, parades, chorus lines, and spinning wheels. Pods crashed into rocks, into lakes, into each other, and the Flopglopple sped over several hillsides in the meantime, still clutching his loops of Rakoor Ram, the vine of grace.

With disappointment he looked back down the hillside at the Micro Techs, who were out of the chase and swearing at each other, blaming each other for the collisions.

"They're fast," remarked the Flopglopple, "but not fast enough." He zoomed away, and very shortly had brought the vines of pliable grace to E.T.

"Did you have any trouble?"

"None," said the Flopglopple.

*　　*　　*

The Rakoor Ram vine was taken into the turnip and shaped into a sphere of interlocking points, nearly as big as the turnip shell itself. The vine had already been soaked in Tadana, and grown steel-like in nature. The robot, looking at the vines, and at the hardened, hollow turnip shell embedded with steely Fusion Blooms, shook his head. "These things are no longer vegetal; they have crossed the border and are hard, technological creations, as I myself am." He looked at E.T. "What science is this, that shapes the plant world so?"

"An outlawed one," said E.T. He too paused and

contemplated his work—this hollow hardened shell, and its new spherical lattice, the vine of Rakoor Ram, twisted like a nest of steel serpents. I have coaxed these plants to densities and strengths beyond their law, and they have obeyed me. Thus, as the robot says, they are no longer vegetal, and I do not know what they really are, only that they are capable of withstanding enormous heat and pressure.

"Now," he commanded, "we must fix Dagon Sabad at each of these twists." He indicated the spots where they'd intertwined the vine into little cups, and into each of these cups a shoot of Dagon Sabad was placed.

"A lovely garden," said the robot, nodding at the spherical arbor. "A perfect decoration you have made in secret, briiiiick cliiiiiick, and we will present it to the Lords of Lucidulum. Is this your plan?"

"Something like that," said E.T.

*   *   *

"It's working perfectly," said Elliott to Michael, as they walked through the school hallway. "I've been playing hard-to-get and Julie's nuts about me." Elliott preened himself proudly. It was almost too easy, this business of becoming a sharp operator. He supposed that he'd go through a series of girlfriends, starting with Julie and ending who knew where?

"Well," said Michael, "don't out-cool yourself."

"Mike, I know what I'm doing. I understand the *moves*."

"Here's my class," said Michael, turning into a doorway. "See you later."

Elliott continued on by himself, toward the basement stairs. Yes, it was easy, this girlfriend routine.

Of course, he still hadn't kissed her, but that was designed to drive her straight into his arms.

Crazed with passion.

How could a guy miss with a plan like that? It was one of life's unfolding answers, the kind that comes to you naturally, if you're patient.

He turned the corner of the hall and saw Julie standing there, talking to Snork Johnson, captain of the junior swimming team, of which Julie was a member. She was leaning back against the wall, and Snork was leaning in next to her, supported by an elbow to the wall, so that his lips were terribly close to hers.

And she was smiling.

The way she smiles at *me*, thought Elliott, the blood draining from his brain. He stared at them, at the angle of Julie's posture, at her silky ponytail, and at Snork's broad shoulders and superior manner. He could swim underwater from here to Japan.

Elliott wanted to step between them and drill Snork Johnson between the eyes. After which Snork Johnson would beat him senseless.

Julie, can't you see I'm standing here?

She did not see him standing there, or if she did, she didn't seem to care.

My *plan*, thought Elliott, as a deep sigh passed through him, like soft slow haunting music heard in the night.

He turned and shuffled in the other direction. Life had just given him another important lesson. There was a fatal flaw in his plan. The girl can find *somebody else*.

He stumbled toward the stairs and started down them. He felt feeble, weak, dizzy, heard a soft trumpet playing a heart-breaking tune in his ear.

Where have I heard that trumpet before?

In Mr. Zontack's living room. She wanted me to dance with her and I was staring at Mr. Zontack's shark.

Julie, he cried inside himself, don't go with Snork Johnson!

He entered the basement of the school, and ducked into the locker room. He'd go into gym class and do 250 chin-ups in preparation for some serious swimming.

Because action was needed.

"Hey, Elliott," said Greg, "how's it going?"

"'kay," mumbled Elliott, and got quickly away. He couldn't talk to anyone, it hurt too much. He raced to the chinning bar, and after twelve fast chin-ups he dropped to the floor, arms trembling.

The gym echoed with bouncing basketballs, and Elliott joined one of the games. His usually laid-back style was suddenly frenzied, and he raced around the court, calling madly for the ball and gunning shots from every angle. In his frenzy, he did not see when an equally excited little replicant of E.T. came through the ceiling. The replicant whirled, spun, was as keyed up as Elliott but as always, was off target.

It landed in assistant coach Munsterweich's gin-filled liniment bottle, from which it emerged still more confused. It shot off, great excitement still propelling it, and crashed into the electric scoreboard, where it clung among the buzzing lights.

El-li-ott, I am carrying forward a great plan!

Julie, sighed Elliott, oh Julie.

In the innermost chamber of Lucidulum, the Contentment Monitor made his report. "My unit investigated the demoted Doctor of Botany."

"And?"

"Though all seemed to be in order, I was not satisfied. I went, therefore, to inquire of Botanicus, chief of the agricultural sector."

"And what did Master Botanicus say?"

"He said the doctor was working on a bug. Apparently one that troubles the ear."

"Good, he is finally doing useful work."

"Yes sir."

* * *

"A dozen ruined pods!" shouted the head of Micro Tech Security. "I send you out to find valuable stolen equipment and you ruin what equipment we own. Junk!" He pointed at the dented, wrinkled, racked-up pods, which now lay in a heap outside Micro Tech Headquarters. The head of Security was hopping about in fury, his eyes bulging, his transparent interior a tornado of temper. "Nincompoops! Imbeciles!"

"Sir, the forest kept jumping around."

"An entire forest jumping around?" screamed the head of Security as he jumped around. "Do you expect me to believe that?"

"Sir—"

"Shut up. Repair those pods! And resume your search!" The head of Micro Security stormed off the field and back into his office, promising himself that whoever had stolen the equipment would pay for all this aggravation. "I'll have him counting stove bolts in Outer Igbolgia."

* * *

E.T. and the Flopglopple carried another plant into the turnip—a large one with thick rubbery leaves. "What is this?" asked the robot.

"It is Rasoor Oob," said E.T., and pointed to the bulbous fruit at the center. "Pierce it."

The robot did so, ejecting a sharp spike from his fingertip, and a membranous substance gushed from the fruit.

"Spread it quickly, before it dries," said E.T., and indicated that the spherical lattice should be covered. They worked until the entire arbor was covered with the membrane and they had an airtight inner space, a ball within a ball. "Rasoor Oob," said E.T., and pressed the membrane with his fist. It was already drying into a firm clear skin. "It can withstand a hundred atmospheres."

*   *   *

E.T. entered his own village again, and made his way toward the family gourd. He found the Parent outside, tending to the herb garden. Each patch of herbs was surrounded by a ring of gemstones, of the sort to which that herb was most in tune; stone and herb grew together, fostering each other's well-being. To the herb the stone gave stored warmth and reflected light, and to the stone the herb gave waves of wisdom, in higher spirals—the wisdom of the rooted, which the stone could mull over in its long eternity of solemn contemplation.

"Hello, my Parent," said E.T., stepping along the little garden path.

"Welcome, child. You have been away at your new greenhouse?"

"Yes," said E.T. "I've created a very large turnip."

"And your ger-a-ni-um? Is that how it is called?"

"Yes, my Gertie geranium. I have caused it to flourish."

"Good," said the Parent. "The blossoms of the universe should be spread. It is the truest diplomacy, for *our soul is in the flower*, as the old writings have it."

The Parent continued puttering in the herbs, straightening, transplanting, its ancient back bent; the herbs responded with the tiniest of movements, not lost to E.T.'s trained eye. "Your garden thrives," he said.

"Ah well," said the Parent, "just a hobby. Nonetheless, these archaic medicines—" It broke off a tiny leaf and breathed the aroma between its fingers. "—they are still the best."

"You are a great healer," said E.T.

"And so, dear child, are you. My lore is yours. What have I not taught you?"

"You have taught me all," said E.T. "And I must apply your teachings." He bent to a tiny patch of emerald herbs and ministered to them as he spoke. "I won't see you again for a while. My new researches shall claim all my attention, night and day."

The Parent looked at him, eyes holding a strange glitter. "What is the medicine for loneliness?" asked the Parent, startling E.T.

"Have *you* such a need?" asked E.T.

"No, child, I have left the rings of fire that burn us with one desire and another. But—have you?"

"I'm uncertain," said E.T. "I have feelings I do not understand."

"The Jumpum is a restless tree," said the Parent. "In that way it has forsaken much of its former serenity."

"But it found the water for which it thirsted," said E.T.

The Parent gazed at E.T. again, and seemed to read E.T.'s soul as easily as looking in a flower's cup. But it said nothing, only placed its leathery palm on E.T's head, and rubbed it gently. E.T. felt as if he were an herb in a tended garden, receiving the healing touch of the well-schooled gardener. The spirals of wisdom appeared to him, and he knew the Parent was raising him one spiral more, to help him in the great task that lay before him.

*   *   *

In the night, then, when the gourd was still and even the Lumens were sleeping, E.T. rose from his bed and walked softly down the neck of the gourd toward the Parent's chamber. He held a single Lumen by a thread, the sleepy Lumen's light flickering on and off as it dreamed.

E.T. entered the chamber. There, stretched out on its own bed, was the Parent, ages old. *I do not even know how old,* reflected E.T. When his own life had begun the Parent was already an Elder, and the aura of such creatures is immense and unfathomable. That aura shone as the Parent slept, and E.T. stepped into its radiance. It affected him all over, and filled him with an indescribable bliss, for the Parent loved him, and it was a wise love born of great time. E.T. could feel intelligence and counsel blending into him, guiding him. He stood motionless in the glow of the teaching, and knew he'd never reach the end of it, for the Parent had comprehended the immortal self.

E.T. looked at the ancient face in repose. So much of what he knew came from this being, and yet when all was said and done this being was a mystery, for the Elders gradually begin to vanish in a mist, their thoughts so inscrutable that they become silent as the trees somehow, and one can pass them by and never know that they are wisdom; so was the Parent vanishing, gaze involuted, silent as wood and stone, and mystery ever increasing.

E.T. himself had begun to feel this mystery gathering in his own form—for he too was changing. His own path had taken such an unexpected turning that he was no longer certain of life's goal, as once he'd been. The goal was mystery, the trail unmarked. And so one mystery faced another—he and the wise Parent, a conundrum. And yet—

He bent over the beloved sleeping form, and touched his finger lightly to the Parent's forehead and whispered, *"I'll be right here."*

*   *   *

Micron entered the turnip, lengths of wire draped over his outstretched arms. The robot followed behind him, bearing the first of many loads of electronic apparatus which the Jumpum trees had been concealing in their roots.

"Not new," said Micron, "but perfectly adequate." He lifted the modular pieces, examining each one carefully and admiring its construction. "Built by my wing, microscopic detail. This single unit—" He held a small box up. "—has two million parts. Here's the main computer, fits in the palm of your hand. Here's the—"

"Can you fit it into our design?" asked E.T. nervously.

"I'm a Techno. You ask us, we make it happen. You've got a nice little shell here. It will stand stress?"

"It is rated above the best alloys," said the robot, as a length of tape clicked from his chin slot, bearing his latest stress measurements of the turnip.

Micron tore it off, looked at it. "This will do fine."

*   *   *

A semicircle of computerized units—the assembled command module—wrapped itself around Micron and the robot, who sat before the many controls, pressing buttons. "Give me fore . . . aft . . . trim," said Micron.

The robot pressed, as instructed, his display board

lighting up. "All functional."

The transparent sphere within the turnip was now a double lattice, of vines and wires, all of it coated by the membrane of Rasoor Oob. Micron pressed one of the buttons on his console, and the mouth of a Fusion Bloom was exposed in the wall of the turnip, a metallic shield dropping away. At once the flower of Dagon Sabad that faced it stirred and spat a tongue of serpentine power into the waiting mouth of the Fusion Bloom.

"Number One firing," said the robot, as the Fusion Bloom roared, plasma streaming through the wall of the turnip, into the outside air.

"Good," said Micron. "Let's try the entire lower ring."

The robot threw a lever, which simultaneously removed the shields from the circle of Fusion Blooms near the floor of the turnip. The nearby flowers of Dagon Sabad quivered, and spat their charge, stimulated by the opening mouths of the Fusion Blooms.

The lower ring of Fusion Blooms roared, in a sound that vibrated the floor of the turnip under E.T's feet. The Flopglopple looked at him. "That is the sound of the ancient world," he said, "when our atmosphere was alive with the primal fire."

Outside, the lizards watched, as the turnip's lower portion was lit in a net of glowing plasma.

"Close main valves," said Micron to the robot. "We don't want to draw any spectators."

*   *   *

"Captain," said a crew member of an intermediate orbiting station. "I've just picked up a tremendous power surge." He pointed to the viewing grid. "A sixth magnitude surge, Zone Twenty-Seven, Lucidulum."

"Relay to the fleet," said the orbiter captain. "There should be no reactors of that magnitude there."

"Orbiter Five to Lucidulum. Reporting Sixth magnitude surge."

* * *

"This is Fleet Commander Lucidulum. Ships One and Two, investigate power surge, Zone Twenty-Seven, over."

"On the way, sir. One and Two."

* * *

E.T. and the Flopglopple entered with two more plants, potted, with enormous leaves and fruits that were quite clearly and rhythmically breathing.

Micron turned in his seat. "Ah, that feels good." He inhaled deeply. "Pure oxygen," he said, turning to the robot, who was belted in beside him. "Those plants give it off in great quantities."

"I regret," said the robot, "that respiration is not required in my system." His mechanical eye-shades fluttered sadly.

"A Moja Vari plant," said Micron, turning to E.T. "Am I right?"

"Breath of Travelers," said E.T., nodding and placing the two plants near the nutrient troughs and tubes that fed Dagon Sabad and which would now also feed Moja Vari. "Two will be sufficient. They reproduce very quickly." He pointed to the seed buds that dotted the leaves, a few of which had already dropped into the soil of the pot and were now sprouting.

The robot turned back to his glowing screen, on which two bright objects suddenly appeared. "Approaching starcraft, high velocity."

Micron popped up and down in his seat, straining against his safety belt. "Those are Lucidulum cruisers! They're after us!" He turned toward E.T.

E.T. lifted a finger. "We must—buzz off."

"We've got no food, no water!"

E.T. pointed to the nutrient troughs and tanks. "Dagon Sabad and Moja Vari are provided for. As for us, we will find *junk food* along the way." He hurried over to the radar screen, where the blips were getting bigger and louder. "Now please—buzz off!"

Micron and the robot activated the command console, pressing many buttons, throwing all the levers. The door of the turnip slid closed, followed by the second door in the membranous inner sphere which the Flopglopple drew shut, the membrane self-sealing.

"All secured."

"Main engines firing."

The lower rings of Dagon Sabad began to quiver, plant after plant stirring. From their centers tongues of fire leapt into the mouths of the Fusion Blooms.

Outside the lizards watched, as the bottom half of the turnip lit up, Fusion Blooms belching plasma. The turnip seemed to hiccup off the ground; then suddenly it was lifted higher, camouflage blowing off it in a swirl of leaves.

In ancient days, said one of the lizards, *there were plants such as this.*

A fine sight, said the second lizard. *The little doctor is wise.*

On all sides, the Jumpum trees began bouncing

around. The sight of the turnip sailing into the air inspired them to mighty leaps of their own, and they accompanied it, briefly, in the air, then dropped away as it continued to climb.

Within the turnip, the robot continued to work his control board. "Second stage," he said, and his large round eyes began to fill with a grid of sparkling constellations, as his internal navigational mode came on.

E.T. went from place to place in the lattice work of Dagon Sabad, as the plant shot forth its power— streams of it flowing and feeding the rocketry of the Fusion Blooms. His turnip ship lifted rapidly now, into the night sky.

The robot switched on the outer viewing screens and the heavens appeared before them. Moving among the stars were two Lucidulum cruisers, rapidly approaching.

*   *   *

Botanicus and E.T.'s Parent sat together in the Parent's gourd, engaged in friendly reminiscing, for they were both old parties, and ancient citizens of the Green Planet. Upon the table before them was ambrosia Botanicus had brought, poured in crystalline cups whose pattern was a network of the distant stars in the constellation of Nahaz Erdu. They clicked their cups together, and the ten fingers of Botanicus glowed at the tips—his wisdom digits, one luminescence for each great deed he'd accomplished, ten in all, in a life measured in eons.

"Your child is unique, dear friend," he said. "He has always been my finest student."

The Parent sighed and sipped the ambrosia. "The Destiny Dreamers saw all this, of course, long ago.

But it was thought better to keep it hidden."

"The best decision," agreed Botanicus. "A great fate is hard enough, without being told of it an advance."

"And naturally," said the Parent, "one hopes that one's child will be spared, that he will remain ordinary, and consequently, happier."

Beside the beaker on the table was a transparent ball, showing the living night sky, stars twinkling. Botanicus leaned toward the ball, keenly interested, his ten fingertips radiant. "He found the power, he applied it correctly. And now—"

Streaking into view within the ball were the images of two Lucidulum starcruisers, and one flying turnip.

* * *

"Briiiiizz . . . starcraft closing fast." The robot's arms moved quickly, working his bank of controls. "I am setting course Six Seven Two, Near Moon Pass."

"Firing upper ring," said Micron, punching a second row of buttons, and another portion of Dagon Sabad's arbor trembled, and spat fire.

E.T. stood beside Micron's seat. "Does it respond?"

"It has kick," said Micron, as the turnip continued to climb. He pressed more keys on his board. "We have a few wobbles, because the power is so raw." He looked over his shoulder at the crackling lattice work of Dagon Sabad. "Where did you find that thing?"

"A rare specimen," said E.T. "It must approve of one's ambitions before it accompanies one."

"Well, let's hope it doesn't change its mind," said Micron.

"I'm feeding it what it likes," said the Flopglopple,

tending the nutrient tanks.

And I, thought the robot, gazing at the Near Moon growing larger in his viewing screen, *I continue my search for truth, I go where it takes me. I go . . .*

*   *   *

"Visual sighting, Captain, starboard."

"Aircraft specification, please," said the captain calmly, as he trimmed to starboard.

"It's—it's—"

"Yes? What did you say?"

"It appears to be a—I'm sorry, Captain, I—"

"Well, speak up, what is it?"

"A flying turnip, sir."

The starcruiser captain swallowed with some difficulty, and switched on his microphone, connecting him with the Commander of the Fleet.

"Starcruiser One reporting. In pursuit of Sixth Magnitude power emitter."

"Aircraft specification, please."

The starcruiser captain sighed, and made his report.

*   *   *

In the innermost chamber of Lucidulum, a startled voice rang out. "A flying *turnip?*"

"Yes, Your Lordship."

"The Commander of the Fleet is pursuing a vegetable?"

"Apparently so, Your Lordship. It appears to be some sort of hybrid."

A soft click on the central communication board sounded. "Commander, this is the Inner Chamber. "You are pursuing a turnip?"

"Affirmative, Your Lordship."

"Do not fail to capture it, Commander. I'll not have our planet circumnavigated by members of the cabbage family."

"Circumnavigation is not its course, sir. It is already at the edge of our gravitational field and still accelerating."

"I don't care where it's going or how. You command the finest spacecraft in the galaxy. *Catch it.*"

* * *

A V-shaped stream of starcruisers climbed, like the point of an arrow, aimed at E.T's vehicle. The root of the great turnip dangled like a tail and its leaves had all blown away; but its network of Fusion Blooms drove it with passionate brilliance toward the Near Moon, plasma flowing from it in a hundred tongues.

But the starcruisers, pride of the galaxy, were gaining, ramjets flaming.

The voice of the Fleet Commander echoed in each of the ships. *"Prepare to deploy meteor nets."*

A hatchway beneath each of the cruisers slid open, and as from the spinnerets of some great spider, lengths of super tensile line were spun out, and held by telescoping rods that joined the lines from cruiser to cruiser, in one great net, strong enough to hold a speeding comet.

Inside the turnip, Micron's fingers were flashing over his command console, increasing power, activating more rings of Dagon Sabad. The robot's metal fingers moved with equal precision at his navigation tasks. This was like the old days, when he was a new machine, flying with the Fleet to the unknown—when

I was young, before they replaced me, before I became outmoded.

He looked at the rear viewing screen, at the pursuing Fleet, the Fleet that had scrapped him. "On course," he said, turning to Micron. "We are headed into the Far Moon Pass."

In the viewer, the Near Moon fell behind and the Far Moon grew increasingly larger. E.T. looked into the view screen and saw the starcruisers deploying their nets. They were trying to catch him, like a bug, and pin his wings forever. He hurried over to the ring of Dagon Sabad, and began to implore the plant to put forth more power. To each flower of Dagon, he spoke soft botanical incantations from his great storehouse of knowledge. "Do wheelies . . . keep truckin' . . . pour it on . . . burn, baby, burn . . ."

"More!" cried Micron as he saw the net closing in on them. "We've got to have more!"

E.T. shuffled nervously back and forth, coaxing Dagon Sabad to pour its true form out, the universal force that quickens the Cosmic Egg, the force stored in this simple unassuming plant. "Please," begged E.T. "Show your stuff!"

To what end? asked the spirit of Dagon Sabad.

E.T. tried to answer, but no language from Earth or the stars could describe what he felt. His heart alone glowed, and from it came many vibrations—of a simple love he'd known, given by a stranger in the universe, a boy, whose soul was somehow the hope of the world. "His love is just a speck of dust in the ages, Dagon Sabad, but I believe it is the only treasure."

Acceptable, said Dagon Sabad.

*   *   *

"Net formation stabilized."

The starcruisers were fused as one craft, their arrow shape inverted now, into a scoop, bearing in on their target. The Far Moon had been passed, and the stars alone were ahead.

The commander, leading the formation, gave the order. "Full acceleration."

"Full power, Commander."

The net closed, encircling E.T's ship. But Dagon Sabad, quickener of the Cosmic Egg, released a burst of seventh magnitude power, which it used for stirring sleeping nebulae.

At his viewing window, Micron saw the stars ahead cluster and shift to the blue spectrum, as the turnip accelerated to light speed and beyond.

"Briiiicck...we have escaped the net. Setting course, constellation Nahaz Erdu, Gate of Dimension."

I've just been outrun by a turnip, said the Commander of the Star Fleet to himself.

"But I can't control it!" cried Micron, tilting off his seat and dangling by his safety belt.

The turnip was wobbling, going into a spin, its walls beginning to shake. They had full power, of the seventh magnitude, but the untried ship, the experimental turnip, was unable to stand up to it.

E.T. fell down with the pitch and slid across the floor. His eyes rotated wildly, as the immensity of the power he'd tried to harness shook him from place to place. "El-li-ott!" he cried, knowing it was over, that his luck had failed, and that he'd dragged his innocent friends to their doom. The Flopglopple's face appeared next to his, as the creature joined him in sliding around.

"Forgive me," said E.T.

". . . lovely time . . . sliding . . ." said the Flopglopple, for whom rolling over a waterfall in a broken barrel would be quite enjoyable, and pitching about in deep space in a rattling turnip was even better.

"We'll be killed!" cried E.T.

"Upside-down!" answered the Flopglopple, as the ship stood him on his head, where he balanced momentarily, toes in the air.

He doesn't understand, reflected E.T. He's a simple soul who trusted me, and now—

Pieces of the wall cracked, fell inward. Wires sparked and burned. The Lumens careened around, their light flickering. E.T. slid the other way across the floor, mind a net of anguish and regret. How had he dared fly in the face of the unknown? There were unwritten rules and he had broken them all. A telepathic surge went out from his brow, containing all that he knew from the collected centuries. It formed a telepathic replicant of tremendous vitality, his last gift to Elliott.

*   *   *

Elliott stood in the shadows of the dance floor, watching the couples doing their thing under the rainbow light. It was Friday night and the community recreation hall was filled. And Julie was dancing with Snork Johnson.

"Guess he beat you out," said Tyler, standing next to Elliott.

"You think I care?" Elliott straightened the lapels of his jacket.

"Yeah," said Tyler, "I think you do."

"Well, you're wrong," said Elliott.

"Cut in on him," said Tyler. "Tell him to paddle off."

Elliott looked at Snork.

If I told him to paddle off, he'd cream me. At the very least, he'd humiliate me with some cutting, superior remark in front of Julie, to which I'd have no reply.

Because Snork has confidence and machismo. Because his father's a judge.

Elliott flashed for a moment on his own father, the missing link, gone, gone, gone. And with him had gone something undefinable, but it translated into confidence.

Of which I've got zero.

Zero charisma.

A wave of loneliness hit Elliott, as he felt the space that separated him from his father, and Julie, and everybody.

"Well," said Tyler, "go to it. Tell Snork to get lost. Tell him if he horns in on your girl again, you'll put a pin in his water wings."

"I'm going downstairs," said Elliott, and walked along the edge of the dance floor, to the door. He went down the narrow staircase to the first floor of the rec hall, where the Ping-Pong tables were. A bunch of guys were there, all of them dateless losers pretending they didn't care, while working on their backhand serve and blasting some wicked shots over the net. When a girl went by they put a little more spin on the ball in the hopes of demonstrating what championship Ping-Pong was all about, and of course the girls didn't pay any attention.

Lance was there, squinting across one of the tables, *Nerd News* rolled up in his back pocket. "Hey, Elliott, how's it going? Come on, I've got this table reserved."

Elliott sighed and picked up a paddle. This was his Friday night, playing Ping-Pong with the world's biggest nerd.

"Alright, Elliott, I've been perfecting my serve."

Elliott returned it lifelessly, not caring, the ball falling into the net.

"Devastating, isn't it," said Lance. "I sense a shut-out in the making." He squinted across the table again and lofted the ball in his special thumb-wiggle serve. It bounced on Elliott's side and skipped over his paddle.

"I'm in incredible form tonight," said Lance.

All along the wall, video games were buzzing, crackling, filling the air with muffled explosions. Overhead the ceiling rumbled with the sound of the dance floor. Julie was up there, part of the sound, part of the music and the mood. While I, thought Elliott, play Ping-Pong with Lance.

"Brace yourself, Elliott, here comes a world class move."

E.T's replicant came through the ceiling, finally on target and streaking toward Elliott's head. It landed, smoothly, merging with Elliott's energic aura, then blending still more deeply, into his innermost nature. Elliott felt a faint ripple pass through him, and flicked his Ping-Pong paddle, sailing the ball back at Lance with a table-edge hit that sent the ball over Lance's paddle and bounced it off his forehead, between the eyes.

The replicant sank deeper into Elliott, down into the most delicate parts of his personality; there the replicant saw a vague and shadowy form, burdened with sadness; it was part of Elliott, the part that weighed him down, that destroyed his poise, and made him wander lonely.

The replicant entered the shadowy form, and dissolved it at the center, scattering its cloudy nucleus. The shadow lightened, then dissolved, and within it was a beautiful sphere of blue, a tiny replica of the Earth carried in each Earth soul. It shone with wondrous beauty, and E.T's replicant circled around it, again and again, scattering the mists of sadness that had enveloped it. And when the beautiful blue ball was shining, the little replicant dove inside it, and curled up there, and radiated the rest of his charge into this core of Elliott's form, this gem at the center of the human condition.

Outwardly, Elliott blinked, and tossed his paddle down. He walked across the rec hall to the steps and went up them. He moved onto the dance floor, and crossed over to Snork Johnson and Julie. Snork saw him and turned. "Get lost, shortstop," said Snork with a sneer, as he spun away.

Elliott stepped between him and Julie. "I'm cutting in," he said.

Snork curled his lip up, a superior remark beginning, dripping with elite sarcasm. And then his eyes met Elliott's, and what he saw there dissolved the words in his mouth and turned them into a stammer, decorated with spit bubbles.

Because Elliott's eyes were filled with an uncanny presence, quite beyond anything Snork Johnson had ever seen. He'd just been out-classed in confidence, and he knew it. He turned and paddled away, wondering what had happened.

And Elliott turned to Julie.

"Hi," he said, as the next record came on over the speakers, a soft slow tune, which led them into each other's arms.

"Gee," she said, "you're a smooth dancer, Elliott."

His body was loose, his movements easy and graceful. He felt he'd blended with the night of rainbow lights—and he knew something, very small and elusive, something he couldn't speak of. But it was intrinsically his, and he realized he could never lose it.

Within him, hidden beyond Elliott's powers of comprehension, the replicant glowed, slowly emanating the charge of E.T.'s last gift, after which there could be no others. For E.T. was doomed, his ship shattering apart in the void. But here, within Elliott's heart at least, were all the memories, the stored wisdoms, the power of E.T.'s love. And slowly the replicant faded, and slowly it died.

*   *   *

"They're out of control, Commander," said the lead Lucidulum pilot. "We'll be able to overtake them again."

"Yes," said the Commander, "yes, I see. Deploy the nets once more." And to himself he thought, I will not be disgraced after all. I will not have to bear forever on my record that I was outrun by a flying turnip.

And he smiled to himself.

And then, inside the turnip, an odd thing happened:

At first E.T. thought it was a puncture in the shell of his ship. A curling wisp of something floated in the air before him, like a little cone of fog. He tried to grasp it, but the turnip pitched madly, and he went sliding once more, across the floor.

When he looked up, the wispy cloud had grown larger and rounder. He pitched back across the floor, sliding with his Flopglopple, and when he looked again, the cloud had grown yet more substantial and was, moreover, now resembling nothing so much as a large bulb of garlic. The bulb moved, semitransparent, ethereal, a walking cloud, toward the command console where Micron and the robot were struggling to maintain control of the turnip. The ghostly garlic bulb stood in beside Micron, and as it did so, it gained final shape, and its cloves unfolded with a metallic gleam, and long sinewy arms extended.

Don't get nervous, you sawed off transistor.

"Sinistro!" cried Micron.

The wraith smiled, and gestured, to a second wisp of ethereal substance forming in the room. *We've projected a bit of our mind power your way.*

The second wisp of mental stuff took shape on Micron's other side; as the wisp gained density, it began hopping up and down like an excited toadstool.

"Electrum!"

At your service, said the old wraith, bending over the control board, his once-bruised umbos now nicely shaped again and shining. Then beside him, a third wisp formed, like a mummy appearing from some buried chamber of the galactical tombs. It was Occulta's wraith, eyes burning with flames of yellow diamonds. *And now,* said his spectral voice, *let's trim this turnip.*

In the viewing screen, the Lucidulum fleet appeared, drew closer, nets deployed. But Sinistro took over the controls, and Occulta and Electrum floated out onto the exterior surface of the turnip, where the

Fusion rockets were blasting.

They separated, one to each side of the turnip, riding on its edge. Then they extended their arms, and a current leapt from their fingertips, sparkling and brilliant, and circled the turnip. Two of these magnetic rings they laid, like the frame of a gyroscope, the currents weaving, spinning, setting up a magnetic balance for the ship, and calming its fearful quaking.

From sun to sun, said Occulta, raising his arms to the stars, *let our rings be charged*.

Then he turned to the pursuing fleet of Lucidulum and gave them a smiling wave, as their ships again fell behind in the chase, lost in the stabilized turnip's exhaust.

"On course," said the robot, inside. "Approaching constellation Nahaz Erdu, Gate of Dimension."

E.T. crawled to his feet, as the constellation appeared on the viewing screen, rushing toward them.

*　　*　　*

The soft song was slowly ending, as Elliott spun Julie to the center of the dance floor, beneath a big glass ball made of hundreds of tiny mirrors. The glass world turned slowly above them, reflecting the rainbow light of the hall, and Elliott drew Julie closer to him, and placed his lips on hers. They kissed, and the colors flashed, and in every facet of the turning world of glass Elliott and Julie were reflected in their first slow, perfect and unforgettable kiss.

*　　*　　*

And here we must leave you, said Sinistro, at the control board, and even as he spoke his ethereal substance began to fade, unable to enter the Gateway of

Dimension. Sinistro became just a wisp of fog again, as did Occulta and Electrum.

"Mind projection fading," said the Flopglopple, as the wisps became no more than thin quivering plumes of disappearing crystals. But E.T. could hear, across the void, Electrum calling:

Don't forget my bicycle!

E.T.'s turnip ship entered the constellation of Nahaz Erdu, flying straight to the wormhole in its center, the Gateway of Dimension.

The turnip slipped from one time-space to another, and emerged at the second lap of its journey, in the Outer Sea of Light. Ahead were other wormholes, by which they would bridge the immensity of the universes, emerging ultimately in the Milky Way.

E.T. looked at his shipmates—Micron, the robot, and the Flopglopple—and held up two fingers, in the V-for-Victory sign he'd learned on Earth, his index finger glowing. And then, suddenly, the other finger lit up, signifying a great deed accomplished.

About the Author

William Kotzwinkle—novelist, poet, two-time recipient of the National Magazine Award for Fiction, and National Book Critics Circle Award nominee—is known for his broad range of style and subject. Among his noted works are *The Fan Man*, *Fata Morgana*, *Queen of Swords*, and *Doctor Rat*, winner of the World Fantasy Award. His stories have been included in *Great Esquire Fiction*, *Redbook's Famous Fiction*, and the *O. Henry Prize Stories*.